FOWLER

WALSH'S LAIR BOOK 1

KATHI S. BARTON

This is a work of fiction. Names, characters, places, and incidents are products of the author's imagination or are used fictitiously and are not to be construed as real. Any resemblance to actual events, locations, organizations, or persons, living or dead, is entirely coincidental.

World Castle Publishing, LLC
Pensacola, Florida
Copyright © 2024 Kathi S. Barton
Paperback ISBN: 9798891261365
eBook ISBN: 9798891261372
First Edition World Castle Publishing, LLC, January 26, 2024
http://www.worldcastlepublishing.com
Licensing Notes
Cover: Cover Designs by Karen
https://www.cover-designs-by-karen.com
Editor: Karen Fuller

The Gathering Storm

~~The Peace of being without war~~
~~Evenness of mind, temper, and composure~~
~~Create by imagination, invention, and design~~

Storm walked around the little store listening to the gossip about one of the biggest disasters ever recorded—at least how these people were now witnessing it. She shook her head in amazement. How could humans be so insensitive? Not to mention stupid. That was one of the million and one reasons that she didn't hang out with humans, too. The rumor mill was running full blast, it seemed today.

"They say that thousands of those bastards are dead. Whole place just split the roads and ate'em right up. Can't you just imagine what they were thinking when they were being swallowed up like that? I can't, I tell you what."

"Heard tell that them there houses just toppled over like the kid's blocks. Smashing people while they slept in their beds." The man speaking shook his head. "Mercy sakes alive. It sure did a nasty bit of business over there on that street."

"God is taking some sort of vengeance on them there foreigners. Sure as I'm a 'sitting here, it's God doing them people in." She actually had to physically close her own mouth when the person made that statement. "They should have stayed in their own place, not here where we people are."

Wondering what they'd say about her and her sister if they knew what they really were made her smile. She wasn't going to speculate on it too much, but they'd have plenty to say. There was no doubt about that.

Storm and her twin sister, Ember, were time adjusters for the world. They moved throughout time and made slight adjustments in the fabric of reality when and where it was needed, smoothing out the lines so that it looked untouched, perfect. They'd been doing it longer than any of the beings in this room had been alive. And they would continue to do so long after they were nothing more than dust in their graves.

To do their jobs, they and a great many others, like the two of them, would travel back and forth, sliding into whatever persona was needed to blend into the world they were in. It took great strength and lots of practice to even attempt what they did for the world. Sometimes, they were the only ones standing between the extinction of mankind and the world being populated at any given time. Storm caught a refection of her face as she walked around the little odds and ends store.

Tall, at just over six-foot, Storm was well-proportioned and athletic. Of course, no one would see that under her long dress and equally long sleeves. Her long dark hair, when not pulled into a tight bun at the back of her head as it was now, hung nearly to her waist in springy corkscrew ringlets.

Her skin, like her sister's, was alabaster and smooth as velvet. The only mark that marred their skin was the tattoo of their kind. It was a dragon that curled around their back, clawed hands seemingly holding onto their shoulders while the tail trailed down their ribs and wrapped around their legs. Storm's on her left leg, Ember's to her right. Their wings spread and covered their arms from their shoulders to their wrists. Smiling at the men when they tipped their hats at her, she put her purchases on the counter and waited her turn to be waited on.

At the moment, Storm was in the year nineteen hundred and twenty-three in the body of a school teacher about to start "schooling" the area children in their reading, writing, and arithmetic. It was the closest body that fit her size when she popped into the time zone. The teacher would have no memories of her being Storm for a bit. There would be a slight accident, a small tumble that would alter her memories. Not that she'd remember Storm and what she had done, but the teacher would recover easily and never be the wiser of what she'd done for her world.

This time, working in this area, it had been a small fix. A mountain had come down on a family that was digging for clay and killed the youngest child. Storm had been tasked to save the child. Her future and that of a great many generations beyond her hadn't been born when she'd been killed. Saving the family, simply making them go to the mountainside later than they had planned, had done the trick. Storm loved it when it was something like this had been.

There were times when whole realities had to

be altered. Generations needed to be moved ahead to save someone. Sometimes, it was to save a being or one of the descendants of a human who was needed in the future. Other times, it was to erase a horrific time in the lives of humans — mostly, it was natural disasters where many deaths occurred. Humans, for the most part, would change up their entire lives, nothing to do with the ones that had been killed because they were witnesses to something so horrific that they had seen.

Other times, the consequences of the disasters were too large and affected too many things when they rippled down through the ages and had to be removed. Something as simple as a house being crushed with their things inside. It could have been the witnessing of a family pet being killed. Any and all things that would alter everything, and it was up to them to repair the damage that had been done.

As Time Displacement Officers, they were there to insure that the shifts were smooth, with no overlapping lines after the time frame was removed or fixed. Storm would watch and event, something that she'd fixed a thousand times to make sure that things were normal. However, gifted humans or small children saw the flaws. It was easily explained as déjà vu. Or a dream, too.

Storm was also there to capture another of their kind and bring him to justice. It was he who had moved the family to the mountain for the one to be killed. And he would have profited off the disaster had she not been there when it unfolded.

His name was Grail. He didn't like being in this room. It wasn't like the room wasn't nice. It was, but when your benefactor summoned you, you did what you were told. Bowing before her when she entered the room — just to piss her off — he stood up when she told him to.

"Do stop. Why must you be so annoying? Someday, you'll be king, and I do hope that someone does the same to you."

He had been altering reality to suit his own personal gain and to profit for a while now, but no one could catch him. She was determined to find and make him pay before he could cause any more trouble. Altering a time line too often would lead to sloppy work and time twitches that people would notice. And that was something that she was afraid of more than anything that she'd encountered in the human world.

Profit and notoriety from their jobs, both of

which were laws that carried the sentence of death if broken, was what he had been doing today. Storm shuddered at the thought of the death he would endure when they took him back to Chilast, their magical realm. Death would not come easily or quickly for one like Grail. He had to know that. So why was he doing this when he knew it was only a matter of time before he was caught?

They didn't have the people to chase after him and keep the world and its people safe. As it was now, they were stretched to the limit. Working from sun up to sun down and all the between time too. It had been so long since she'd had a day off that she wanted to just lie down, pull some leaves over her, and go to sleep for about a thousand years.

Storm's twin sister, Ember, had gone to Tokyo to study and gather names of their kind for the continuation of their race. So far, all she'd been able to find was the list of dead. All of the dragons that had come after her and a few others that had been killed. That wasn't doing any of them a bit of good, and they all knew it. They were aging out, the lot of them, and there wasn't anything that they could do about it.

It didn't bother their kind when they would

wind time backward. It was the moving of time forward that would harm them. Time, it would add, even if it was only a click of a second to their age. And having to look at something over and over, forward and back, it might well add as many as ten minutes onto their long lives. After a while and all those adding up, a dragon would age quicker, worn down by time and effort.

Storm had been sent to the Americas for her assignment to find and collect Grail before he could act on his plan. If they didn't find him and, soon, all the others would be useless. They'd all be dead, and there wasn't anything that could be done about it.

But she had a feeling this time was different. They knew his plan, what he had needed, and who to make himself get away. It was what they had needed, what they were counting on to bring him to heel and to make all their lives safer without him in their worlds.

There was supposed to be a natural disaster, a large-scale shift in the earth's interior make up that would cause the entire state of California to drift into the deep ocean and sink, killing all the inhabits there. There were people there that he needed to complete the next phase of his power play against his own kind. She had been sent there to witness this and to bring Grail to the Laws of the Realm.

These people, men, and women alike, were the pioneers of the future that Grail was manipulating. Their collective knowledge would be passed down to their children and then on to the next generation. They were brilliant and would revolutionize the world with Grail's backing and help. And not in a good way that would benefit only themselves and no one else.

They, like Grail, were evil and only thought to gain untold riches and wealth from sources within the different time lines that he was supposed to care for. From future records, the Time Displacement Office – the TDO and the Elders of their kind, knew that he had taken this opportunity to steal them away along with all their equipment. In the aftermath of the devastating slide, everyone would assume they had been killed as well. After decades of exhaustive tracing and retracing the lines of time back, the TDO knew this was where he made his first move to bring his plan to fruition.

But the quake, the distraction as it was, never happened. At least not where it had occurred in the history they had studied. It had happened the day before in Tokyo, where Ember was researching and gathering information. She worried for her, and when she couldn't contact her, she knew the worst had happened.

Storm had been trying to contact her sister for hours without luck. They were both immortals and could shift and fly away if danger was imminent, but with the suddenness of the quake in Tokyo and the horrific scale on which it had occurred, Storm feared her sister needed her and needed her now.

Storm felt the first touches of Ember as she exited the store. The feelings got stronger the more Storm concentrated on her sister's touch to her mind. It was all she could do to keep an eye out as to where she was going and thinking about her sister at the same time.

"Are you all right? I've been trying to reach you for hours. What's happened?" Storm said as soon as the link was snapped into place between them. Ember told her that she was fine, never better. "I've been so worried about you that I can barely breathe."

"There are signs of him here. I have contacted several of our kind in the area, and they say that he stayed with them for one night two days ago. I can smell him and his poison here deep within the belly of the mountains where the records are kept." Storm smiled at her greeting. Ember was never one to mince words when it came to their jobs.

"Did he hurt any of them? Ask them for their help?" It would be just like him to murder them all just to throw them off his scent. But, at least for now, he only killed when he could gain from it.

"No. He spoke to no one but the people that were kind enough to allow him to rest. They say that he had a satchel with him, but he didn't seem to want to let anyone know what was in it. The Elders found a small thread, or we may not have known that he was even here. He's either getting better at hiding from us, or we're getting worse at our job, Storm."

"It's the same story here. He spent a night with the others here and then left. No one mentioned a satchel, though. He moved the place and altered the fabric where he had been. Ember, he didn't take the people he had before. Somehow, he has modified the events of that night yet again." Storm was suddenly terrified, and she was sure things were going to get worse before they caught up with him. "What do you suppose was in the satchel? I mean, is it important, you think?"

"Moran, the one who was closest to him when

he was here, said that it had photos in it. Some of them were old tin types, others digital, and one was a hologram. He thought they looked like me, but the eyes were the wrong color. I'm assuming that it must have been of you. Also, from what I could gather, there were images of the people in California. There… there was a picture of a man, as well. One that we've not encountered in all our searches as yet."

"Photos? Maybe he's using outside help trying to find these people. Makes sense that he would have pictures; he'd have to show them who to look for, right? No, he didn't take anyone, as far as I can tell. It's…he's changed everything again."

There was a long pause through their connection; Storm could feel her sister's tension.

"What is it? Something has happened. Tell me."

"The Elders, they called to me two days ago. They needed an extraction. I…they had me take a human away from a deadly shooting. I've no details yet, but he is to be guarded at all costs. I have him deep within the mountains with us. He is curious but not frightened. I think that is why there was a shift in the location of where the quake happened. I think we missed this man somehow, and we angered Grail by taking him. He was in one of the photos in Grail's collection. Storm, this man, he was to die."

"Who is he? Had he been taken by Grail before? Is he one of Grail's minions?"

"No. He isn't like that. His mind and body are pure. His spirit is clear. The shooting I took him from killed the others like him – men who uphold the law. I barely made it to him before the killings began in a house in New York. My wings were damaged slightly; I've been in a healing sleep until now." Still, Storm could feel her hesitation.

"Tell me the rest, Ember." She could have looked, she supposed, but in her current state, she knew that she'd hurt her sister. And she didn't want to do that. Hurting her would hurt her as well. "Ember?"

"I've been...the others here, we've...I've formed a bond with one. I've found my mate, Storm. After all this time, I've found my mate, and I'm afraid. Not of him, no but what this is going to mean for the two of us. They will curtail my work soon."

Storm felt her heart stutter to a stop. Her mate, Ember, had found her mate. Storm moved to the outer wall of the store and leaned heavily against it. This would change everything. Ember could no longer help her with their job. As soon as Storm thought about it, she felt horrible. Ember had found her mate. She should be rejoicing.

"Storm, please don't be mad. I didn't mean for this to happen." She had hurt her anyway. The tone of Ember's voice told her that.

"Don't be ridiculous. I'm happy for you. It's just a surprise, that's all. I wish you nothing but happiness and good fortune. I love you." Storm, stronger now because she had heard from Ember and knew that her sister was going to be all right, continued. "I'm going to contact the Elders and see what they want me to do now. You'll be all right for now? You're making sure that you're all safe while you work?"

"Yes, I am fine. Thank you, Sister. I will be waiting for you in our cave. You let me know when you will be arriving, and I'll be watching the sky for you."

Storm hoped it would be that easy, but knowing the Elders as she did, she doubted it very much. They would want something from her, and she'd do it because Storm was loyal to a fault.

~~Devotion to the continued existence of life~~
~~Devotion to the supreme good~~

~~Pure condition of body and mind~~

It was against the Laws of the Realm to appear before the Elders in any other form than the one that you had been born to. As soon as Storm arrived at the castle, she reached out to touch the magistrate to set up a meeting with the Elders and the Queen. She was both surprised and terrified that they had readily agreed to see her as soon as she had eaten and shifted.

Food was brought to her, and she enjoyed a large meal. As soon as she had finished, she knew that she needed to complete her mission and get back to her sister. Moving to the outdoor paddock just outside her suite of rooms, Storm began her shift.

She loved to be a human. Storm loved the soft textures of their skin, the feel of the hair upon the body. She also loved the way the fingers bent and was able to grasp things within them. The light feelings of simply walking would make her giddy with anticipation of stepping into the grass or sand with her bare feet. But to be her true self, there was nothing better.

Storm was a dragon, an Enneahedral Dragon — also known as a Ninefold Dragon. She was as rare as any being could be. Storm was the ninth daughter of nine daughters for nine generations. When she had been hatched, she had inherited all the elementals of the earth and the nine directives as well. Her powers were nine times that of her sister Ember — even though she'd only been seconds behind her in coming out of her shell and abilities that went beyond any other dragons.

With being the ninth in so many lines, Storm was to be Queen of their kind as soon as she found a mate worthy of her and her love. But she was in no hurry to find either. She was too busy to care for a lover and didn't want one slowing her down either.

As soon as she stepped into the magical arena, she let her body respond to the pull of her Dragon. First, her body elongated, her spine curving and pulling, stretching to accommodate the large bulk of her form. Then her feet, dainty and small as a human, they too stretched, and great claws formed at the toes. The wings at her back began pulling away from her body and forming into a great expanse, wide and full. Flapping them once, she felt the blood surge through them, and then she pulled them tight against her body. Her face molded and formed into a massive head, teeth a foot in length and sharp as the talons at her feet filled her mouth full and lethal. The human skin along her arms became scales of great strength, able to protect her from any weapon, small or large. Her scales shimmered in the moonlight, catching and reflecting the gold and silver that blazed within each protective shell. By the time the shift was complete, Storm was a massive twenty-five feet tall, seventy feet wide with her wingspan, and weighed several tons of pure muscle and bone. She moved to the large door that went directly into the throne room and bowed before the other dragons gathered there, careful of every step that she took.

"Mistress Storm, thank you for coming to see us so quickly. We have much to discuss." Storm dipped her head to hide her confusion. They had expected her?

"You must go to China. We need for you to bring back the man Alexander Walsh. It is imperative that he survives. He is vital to the future of our race, to all of us."

"Pardon me, Sire, but my sister, Ember, she is—" Storm started to tell them what she was sure that they already knew, but they cut her off.

"Ember is going to have a hatchling soon. She must stay hidden. If Grail finds her, he will destroy her and the babe. No, it is you who needs to go and bring him back to us. May we count on you to serve us well, Mistress Storm?"

"Of course." Storm bowed before them and took a step back to leave the room. She was stopped by a slight cough from behind her.

"My lords, have you yet told the Mistress what is expected of her?" Storm startled. The being was small but by no means diminished in her stature. Standing before her was the strongest being any had ever known. Her mother, Queen of the Enneahedral Dragon clan, had swept into the room, her strength preceding her. "I will take it upon myself to do that now. You're dismissed." The people in the room disappeared at her command.

"Mother, you look well." Storm never knew how to speak to her mother, Morning. She had always intimidated her. Now was no different. Her beauty was one of the reasons; the other was that her mother wasn't really the affectionate sort of person. But then, neither was she.

"You look beautiful, child. I would like for you to shift and meet me in my private chamber. I should like to speak to you about this mission." Nodding once, her mother smiled. "We'll have a luncheon, you and I. And tea. I should like to speak to you about your other adventures, too, if you would allow it."

Immediately, Storm's body started its shift to human form. Within seconds, she was dressed similarly to her mother in a long silk robe with their crest blazing over their hearts. Storm nearly stepped back from her, as Morning was standing very close. Surprisingly, Morning reached out and hugged her close to her.

The tightness of the hug had tears fill her eyes. It had been forever since her mother had hugged her, much less had hugged her first. Wrapping her arms around her mother, she heard her soft sob, and when she pulled away, her mother turned her back to her and started talking. As if nothing had happened.

"This man, Alex, you will bring him back to us safe. It's important." They were seated in the large room that her mother used when she came to the castle's offices. "I know that your sister is there, but she is breeding now. Thank the gods, and it's important to all of us that she be able to deliver her hatchling safely." Her mom sat down, so Storm did the same in an equally ornate chair.

It was not a question, but Storm answered her anyway. "Yes. You can trust me to keep him safe."

"It's not his safety that I worry about. It's

yours." Morning shifted on her seat. Unease was evident on her face and posture. "Alex is your mate. It is determined by the Elders that he will father the next line. His bloodline is strong and pure. He will provide you with love and companionship for the rest of your life and on into the next. You and he and the family you breed will be the ones to destroy evil."

Storm looked sharply at her mother. No. No, this could not be happening. She did not want a mate chosen for her. She stood and began pacing the room.

"You're angry. I don't blame you, I would be—"

"Pardon me, but you don't know me well enough to judge my anger. I will bring this man to you, but no one is choosing my mate." She turned on her mother, not sure that this was a smart move on her part, but she was pissed. "Was Ember's mate chosen for her as well? I'm sure that she'll be thrilled to know that her life has been arranged for her."

"No, her finding her mate was a surprise to us all. But this man, Alex, he's been chosen as your mate since before he was born. And you will not use that tone with me, young lady. I am still your mother." Storm took a deep breath and then sat down when her mother asked her to.

"I miss said what he was to you, Storm. No one chose him for you. It was written in the tomes of the future. You will mate with him and bring children into this world that will be needed. When I said chosen, I meant that it has been written."

She stalked out of the room and into the courtyard again. This time, she shifted as she ran, her body forming and shaping as she went. By the time she had gone a hundred yards, she was launching herself into the sky and soaring across the night.

~~Enjoy great happiness~~
~~Maintain a fond hope for all kind~~
~~Uphold the reparation of magical energy requirements~~

Storm shifted to a human as she touched the ground. Her body threw off its form as if it were a heavy coat she no longer needed. She had landed close to the mouth of the cave where the man Alex was waiting.

Storm had contacted Ember when she left the Realm late last night. Telling her the events that had happened at the castle, but she left out the part of "the man" being her mate. She did not plan on taking him as her mate, so she felt no reason to relay the news. Storm had also asked Ember to have the man waiting for her at the mouth of the cave. Storm did not want to take the time to go down and get him. The sooner she took him to the Elders and finished this assignment, the happier she would be.

"You're to come with me. I'm to take you to the Chilast," she said when she saw who she assumed was Alexander. She put out her hand to have him come with her.

"I don't think so. Not until someone explains to me what is going on. One minute, I'm on a domestic violence call. The next, I'm being wrapped in wings and brought here. Wings—I've seen some weird shit as a cop, but wings are something I've never encountered before." Alex sat hard on the stone next to the wall. He looked stubborn and formidable. She was annoyed but impressed, too.

He was a very handsome man and taller than her by a good half a foot. His hair was dark, as dark as Storm's, but where hers was curly, his was straight and hung just past his shoulders. The shirt he had on had been torn, so she had a delicious view of his hard abs and harder chest. It looked smooth, and her fingers itched to touch, not just his chest but his entire body. Storm decided that she did not like him and would not be his mate, no matter what anyone said about it.

"I don't have time to explain, so get ready to go." She could feel the attraction to him, and she hated him all the more for it.

Before he could say anything else, the earth shook beneath them. Alex fell to the cave floor, and Storm was thrown to the wall, striking her head hard. While she fought the blackness tying to consume her, she threw a protective shell around Alex.

"Well, hello, Storm. You have something that belongs to me. I want him. Now!" Grail moved into the mouth opening of the cave, and Storm felt his power surge against the spell she had wrapped around Alex. It wouldn't work, of course, she was much stronger than him, but it would weaken her more in protecting the human.

Grail had been a gray Dragon in color when Storm had first met him, his color bleeding into his human form, giving his eyes and hair the same rich colors. Now, he was black as pitch. His eyes, once a soft, rich, pewter color, were now black with his dark magic and evil. He was tall, as were all their kind, but he was also heavy. His lack of physical activity not keeping him in the shape he should have been. Though his face, dusky in pallor, was gaunt and shallow. She wondered how he could fly, much less take flight.

"You can't have him. I'm to take him back to the realm." She opened her magic and pushed hard back.

Grail raised his hands, and power appeared in the form of a ball of electricity. The longer he held it, the bigger it grew. If he hit the protection, he would destroy it. Storm needed to get them to safety now.

Storm moved in a flash to stand in front of her assignment; she shifted part way, and her wings fluttered out from her back. She flapped them once, and their powerful movement moved air strongly around the forest and knocked Grail to the ground as he stood in his fragile human form. Turning to Alex, she grabbed him up and ran to the lighted opening just beyond Grail. As she passed him, she felt a searing pain in her back but did not slow her pace. By the time she was in the open light, she was a full dragon, Alex tucked tightly in her talons. She soared high in the air just as Grail screamed at her to come back.

As a dragon, she could see all the areas where it would be safe for them to land. Her vision was perfect, and she could see the heat from any humans or animals below them, not wanting to land where anything could find them. Storm knew she was losing blood, but until she landed and got the man to safety, there was little to nothing she could do. She was getting weaker and knew that she would need to land soon or risk falling and crushing the man she was sent to protect.

Opening her mind, she hoped to be able to speak to the man. It was the way of their kind to be able to talk to their mates when there had been no bond at all between them. Unlike most species, she could have spoken to Alex since his birth had she known about him being what he was to her.

"Are you hurt? I should have asked sooner, but I wanted to get you out of harm's way."

"No. I'm fine. Your claws are digging into me, but I fear that if you lessen your grip, I feel I'll fall to the earth—unless that is your plan? Tell me, Storm, do you plan to play toss the man into the air and see if you can catch him before he plummets to the earth. If so, could we not play today? I have a very busy schedule tomorrow, and if I'm crushed… well, it could put a crimp in things. No, I think a little pinching is preferable to death. I can smell your blood. How hurt are you?" She told him that she was, but she would heal when they landed. "If there is anything I can do to help you, please let me know. I'm pretty handy to have around."

She smiled at his sense of humor. Storm had not expected that. He was being very calm for a man who was being flown well above the clouds by a huge blue dragon.

"I must land soon to sleep and heal. I know of a place where you'll be safe until I can do both. No one will bother you there." She told him with as much reassurance as she could. Weakness was pulling hard at her, and she did not think she could go much longer.

"So you plan to leave me? I hope you don't expect me to sit around quietly waiting for your return. I may not know what is going on or why that other…what was he anyway?"

"He's a dragon like me. And you will stay where I tell you. You are to live at all costs. I don't have time to placate your feelings, human. I can easily say that you were eaten by Grail as not. Now be quiet." Storm began her decent.

Pain racked her body, and she knew that the landing was going to be hard. Seconds before she hit the earth, she dropped Alex and tumbled over him, careful not to land on him. As much as he irritated her, she did not want to kill him.

Her body shifted as soon as she stopped rolling, shifting to the last shape she had taken, hiding her true identity from anyone who would come upon her injured body. It was there to provide their kind with surreptitiousness.

Storm sat up just long enough to ensure that Alex was all right, her body and mind already pulling her to sleep. The area where she had taken them was hers; it was safe and hidden well from everyone, including any of her kind. She saw Alex stand and stride toward her just as blackness pulled her under.

~*~

Alex leaned over the woman he had carried into the house he had found a mile or so from where she had fallen. The fire he had lit in the deep fireplace reflected off her face, the reds and golds of the flames casting surreal shadows across her flawless cheeks. She was a beauty, just like her sister, Ember.

There was no doubt to him that the two women were sisters, as they were identical twins and as alike as any he had ever seen. He moved the dark hair away from her face and ran his fingers down her downy cheek. When she stirred slightly, he grinned.

She was by far the most stubborn person he had ever met.

"Why do you look at me like that?" She looked up at him, her voice soft in the hushed room.

"I was thinking about how unlike your sister and you are. You are very beautiful, both of you. But you lack her softness and the...genteel nature that she has. You are strong and stubborn. And I've never wanted to kiss anyone more than I do you."

The expression on her face was priceless. He nearly laughed out loud but caught himself before it burst forth. He was afraid she would hurt him. Alex was not a stupid man; he had seen what she was, and while it was hard to believe, he was not going to dismiss the fact that she had flown them away from trouble.

"Why?" He asked her what she meant. "Why would you want to kiss me? It's not like I'm all that much. I'm, well, at least for the moment, just a woman who has the ability to change into a great dragon. Nothing special about that."

"Why would I want to kiss you, or why do I think you're stubborn?" He touched her again. He could not seem to help himself. "And you are extremely special. I've only just thought of this too.

You're extremely special to me for some reason. Do you know why?"

She looked at him for long moments, and he suddenly felt her touch his mind again, this time in a searching way, not to speak. Alex was not sure why he did not block her, but he would not try to fight her if she needed reassurance.

"You're a vampire. They didn't tell me that." She sat up on the side of the bed, but he didn't move back. It put them closer than before, and he was happy with that.

"Yes, I'm a vampire. You're a dragon. I didn't know that you even existed until I met Ember. You say 'they'. Who? And who is that man who tried to kill us?"

"The Elders of our kind, they are the ones who sent me to bring you back to them. The other dragon, his name is Grail. He's also a dragon like me, a time shifter. Did Ember tell you what we do?" He nodded, and she continued. "He was there to kill you and me because we're supposed to be mates. We are to deliver the next line of dragons. Mother told me that our children were meant to destroy him and his reign. I didn't stick around long enough to hear why. Grail has been building his power base for many years and has been moving through time, making adjustments in the fabric of lives to gather monies to fund his cause — to destroy all dragons but himself. I was in the Americas waiting for Grail to make a move to take a group of scientists away before they were to die, but he came here to get you instead. We had been tracking him for some time. The earthquake that happened in China was the result of him having a temper tantrum. Ember said that she had been sent to save you, but she didn't know why until I spoke to her. You see, you were to die in that last call you went on when on patrol. When Grail realized that you had survived, he unleashed his anger on those people."

"I'm sorry for them. I never meant to cause them harm." He was a good cop, and he never pulled his gun unless it was the only thing left for him to do.

Storm stood up and looked at him. The glow from the fire danced in her eyes. When she licked her lips, he watched, mesmerized by the pink tip moistening her lush lips. "Storm..."

Before he could claim her mouth, he felt himself being tossed across the room. Storm landed across his body, protecting him from falling debris. Her hand clamped tightly across his mouth when he started to speak.

"Grail." She said in a way of explanation. Moving quickly, she stood and pulled him close to her.

"I know you're in there, Storm, my dear. Come out and play with me, and bring our tasty friend along with you. We'll char him up and laugh over the silliness of all this fighting. I can offer you so much more than he could ever."

Alex pressed back against the far wall and flipped Storm around so that her back was now where his had been, and he moved hard to her body.

"As a human, is he as mortal? Will he die like a regular man?" Alex moved the thoughts through her mind. The words where fast and hard, urgent even.

"No. Yes. It needs to be silver through his heart, though. But his dragon would protect him by wrapping himself around Grail and taking him away. Grail would sense your movement, and as quick as you are, Grail is much faster. You can't...you can't think to beat him, do you? He'll take you, kill you."

"Do you care, Storm? Would you morn me if he kills me?" Now, his voice was a caress, a stroke along her heart and mind.

Without hesitation, without speaking in his

mind, she answered. "Yes. Yes, I would."

"You are mine, understand?" He warned her. At her nod, he kissed her quickly and pulled his gun from his ankle holster. Winking at her, he took her hand and moved to the front of what had once been a small house.

"Please, Alex, please don't do this. He'll kill you." She whispered in his mind again.

"He'll try." When he started to step away, she pulled him back into the semi-darkness. "What?"

"You need to feed from me. I'll strengthen you, protect you. Feed from me, and my dragon will know you, and it'll keep you safe, keep us both safe."

Alex looked at her and smiled. He felt his fangs drop into place to feed. The need to sip from her nearly staggered him off his feet.

He wanted to savor her, make her his, and knew from her sister that dragon blood, especially Storm's blood, was poison to those who did not ask and were given permission before drinking. But for those who had been allowed that rare sip, the benefits were amazing. Alex leaned into her throat, nuzzling her skin, tasting her with his mouth and tongue. Licking the area just over the pulse pounding in her neck, he pulled back slightly and stuck his bite deep and quick. Her moan ran along his skin like a caress.

At the first taste of her essence, he immediately felt the power surge into him. The more he drew from her, the stronger he felt his body getting. Alex was an older vampire, so his strength was not paltry, but with her surging through his veins, he felt extraordinary.

Pulling back reluctantly, he sealed the tiny wounds with a flick of his tongue. Moving his mouth along her jaw, he reached her mouth and sealed his over her heat.

"I know that you're in there, Storm. I demand that you come out now and face me. I have plans for us, plans that do not include that vampire mate of yours. Children of our union will bring me more money than I ever imaged."

Alex backed away from her slightly and saw the lust in her eyes. "If you stay right here, I'll take care of him, and we can get back to where we were before he interrupted us."

"I need to keep you safe. I need to stand at your side." He smiled at her possessive tone.

Moving and taking her hand once again, he hid his gun behind him as they walked forward.

"Ah, the future Queen and her stud. You know,

I think I'm going to enjoy killing him. Oh yeah, this is going to be..."

He never finished. As he dropped to the ground, Grail stared at the smoking gun in Alex's hand.

Alex and Storm watched as Grail began to shift quickly into several forms before he just simply melted into the ground; his blue blood stained the ground beneath him.

There was a lot to be said for the element of surprise.

Chapter 1

Fowler didn't like being in this room. But being summoned here meant that he had to be here. It wasn't like the room wasn't nice. There were plants and flowers in every corner and space in the room. The colors, earth tones that seemed to bring the outdoors into the room and made it feel like a huge open space. Even the paintings on the walls, all of them by famous people who came from his realm, graced the walls in a way that made it all seem seamless in the way they fit together.

It was beautiful, for lack of a better term. Homey would work, too, but beautiful worked the best. He still didn't want to be there. However, when your grandmother summoned you, you did what you were told. Bowing before her when she entered the room—just to piss her off—he stood up when she told him to.

"Why must you vex me so much, Fowler?" He said that it was what he lived for. "Someday, you'll be king, and I do hope that someone does the same to you."

"I can only hope, Grandmother, that it is a long way in coming as I have no desire as yet to take over for my mother. She is doing a great job as queen, as I'm sure you did before her." She huffed at him and then hugged him when he stepped up closer to her. "How have you been? I'm thinking that you enjoyed your trip to the European countries. You look as fresh as an apple hanging on the tree."

"You should be using that considerable charm on a woman instead of wasting it on someone like me. Are you even looking for your mate, Fowler? She is out there. I've told you this before." He grinned at her and told her what he'd been doing. "My goodness, Fowler, you embarrass me all the time."

"Well, as I said, I want to be perfect in the ways of sex when I meet her. So, daily, I find myself a woman, and after wooing her, I take her to my bed and show her everything I learned thus far. Some of them are teaching me — you do want me to satisfy my mate when she comes, don't you, Grandmother?" She huffed at him again. "You do that well. I think you might be better than Melbourne. He did teach you that, didn't he?"

"I doubt that he's taught me much. I am older than the lot of you by a great many years." The two of them stopped speaking when one of the many people who worked at the castle came into the room. There were cookies and scones on a platter, as well as hot tea for his grandmother and a glass of tea for himself. Picking up his glass to taste what he knew would be perfect, he sighed a heavy sigh when he tasted that it had been sweetened by just enough fresh honey. "I've brought you here for a reason, Fowler. I will also say that I wish you would come visit me even if I don't summon you. I miss you boys now that you're out on your own."

"I will make it here more often if that's what you wish. I do so love coming to visit you, Grandmother. You're a hoot." She scowled at him, but it didn't reach her eyes. She loved him and all his brothers more than he thought she did her own daughters. "What is it that I can do for you? You know that I would move the earth for you. You're my favorite grandmother."

"I'm your only grandmother, you imp. And it's serious now. Grail has been moving about the world, making trouble." All thoughts of anything else in his mind scattered. He'd heard of Grail his entire life and what he'd been doing before he and his brothers had been born.

"I thought that dad had killed him." She told him what she knew. "So he's been in hiding healing. Does anyone else know that he's still alive? Mom or Dad know?"

"No. I've only just been made aware of it a few hours ago. Today, I did some research on him and found that he'd been sleeping the sleep of healing all this time. That healing sleep made it appear as if he were dead, and that is why we thought him no more. The reason that I'd never been able to find him until now is that he was in a cave lying upon stone so that no one could feel him." He set his glass down and thought about what she was telling him. "He's not as strong as he once was, but he is gaining strength from those around him. Grail is back to his old ways, gathering an army to kill off all dragons but himself. We cannot allow that to happen, Fowler. If there are no dragons, there is no magic to be had."

"I've thought of this before, but I haven't had the opportunity to ask. If he destroys all dragons, won't that make him weaker in comparison too? What will happen to him if the magic of us all is gone?" She snapped her fingers, and a book appeared in her hand. Handing it to him, Fowler ran his hand over the cover. "I've never seen this before. Is this made of dragon skin?"

The cover wasn't beautiful, but it was soft. Once he touched it, it changed colors, much like the heat of his hand had something to do with it. He'd bet anything that the person who wrote the book they were the one who had bound it and covered it. Even the binding down the side was made of dragon internals; the stomach of a dragon was something that could never be cut or harmed. It was why their kind lived for so long.

"It is. It's the book of Enneahedral. It contains every birth and death of all our kind and the things that have been discovered about us as the years go on. It's magically put in there so that it's done at the time of the event. You and your family and your brothers are the first ever dragons born of a human and a dragon. There is much on your birth, especially that I think that you should familiarize yourself with. It will help you in the coming years. It's been in my possession for so many years that I've lost count." He asked her why he was only just now learning about it. "Because it really is time for you to find your mate. She is out there, Fowler, and she and you will do our kind proud when—"

"Grandmother, we've spoken about this before. I wish to remain unmated because I don't want to have someone used against me when I someday become king. You know what it did to my parents when they were harmed." She said that she did and thought that his father still hurt from it. "He does. The dragon that took him meant to kill him to bring Mom to heel. It nearly killed them both when he was returned to us, having had so much damage done to his body and soul. I will take a mate on, but I won't be king if I do. It's as simple as that."

"Nothing is as simple as that, young man." Her anger blew over him. The heat of it burned deeply into his face and arms. He would heal, but the pain of it, making her upset, was more than his heart could take. "You will do as you're told and find your mate. I have decreed it."

Fowler stood up and bowed before his grandmother. Leaving quickly, he didn't say another word to anyone as he made his way from her chambers to the realm he'd been born to. Going to his home, his anger as palatable as hers had been, Fowler went to the sublevels of his home and began working on the exercise equipment there. Thankfully, it had been magically enhanced so that he didn't break anything as he worked out, or there would have been a great deal of broken and damaged pieces all over the floor.

By the time he'd showered and had some dinner, he was still pissed, but he'd been able to work out most of his anger on the punching bag downstairs. When his mom asked if he'd come to dinner, he asked her if she'd spoken to Grandmother.

"I have. But that's not why I would like you to come over for dinner. There are a couple of things that I need from you. Nothing big, just some of the things that are in the storage lockers that we have that I'd like to clean out. Your brothers will be here too." He asked her if she was going to bring up him finding a mate. "I agree with you on that. You should find her at your own pace. I have no desire to pressure you into anything, Fowler. I've told you the story about meeting your dad. I'm not unhappy with the results of their manipulating things, but I was pissed off that they did it. I would like for you to find your mate, Fowler. Don't get me wrong, but it should be on your own terms and not that of a legend that was written well before your time. Tell me you'll come to dinner."

"I'll be there." He felt better knowing that at least someone was on his side. Dad would want him to find a mate right away. He said that it changed his world and life to have Mom in his life and that having his sons was like icing on the cake. Dad was a romantic and had been all their lives.

Dad was forever buying Mom flowers and candy that made her happy. Once, when he'd been about ready to leave home, Dad had booked a cruise for the two of them to go on while he moved out. So as not to upset her that one of her own was leaving the nest, so to speak. When they returned, he'd been moved out, and his mother was so happy with the cruise that it bothered her very little. He loved watching his parents dance around the kitchen while they were having a good time.

After changing his clothes for something nicer, he made his way to his parents' house. Dad greeted him at the front door with a bear of a hug, and Fowler returned it. That was something else that he loved about his parents was that they were the most affectionate couple he'd ever met. He was the first of his brothers to arrive and was glad for that. He asked his mom about the book that Grandmother had given him. She didn't seem to know much about it.

"I've heard of it, of course. I never looked or asked for it, so that might be why. Ember might know a bit more about it than I do. She was forever looking for something to read when we were growing up." He said that he'd ask her about it. "Also, there are some things that I wanted to talk to you about that are going on in town. Did you know that the mayor is thinking of retiring? Also, I've heard that the high school is going to have to be torn down due to it not being up to code any longer. I think that you and your brothers all went to that place. Not really, but it is old. I think that it was built sometime in the early part of the century. I would guess that it wouldn't be up to code, would it."

"I have looked into the mayor. It's about time that he retired. He's not been a bad person, but he's nearly eighty years old and a bit back in the times for anything new to be happening around here. I don't know that he's even able to use a cell phone. I'll look into seeing who we can get to replace him if you want me to." She said that would be great. "Now that I think about it, maybe Edgar would be a good replacement. He is the most current on his law degree."

"I already asked him about it, and he turned it down. He said that he didn't want to be stuck in an office all day long pushing paper around. I'll speak to him again about it. What about the school? Have you looked into it?" He said that he'd not, as he'd not been approached about it. "I'll leave that up to you as well. I know that there is a woman, I can't remember her name, who is advocating that the school be torn down and have another one be built in the same place. I don't know that there is enough land there to build something that big with parking lots. More and more kids are driving to school, from what I've noticed."

"We own a great deal of land just outside of town that we could do something like that with. I'm not saying that we give it to the town, but perhaps we can work out a deal that makes it so that we still own it, and they sort of rent it for hardly nothing." She said she liked that idea and would set up a meeting with the woman. "I'd like to go with you if you'd not mind. Just so if she has any questions about the land and building, then I can have that ready."

"Perfect. I like that idea better." As his brothers showed up one at a time, they had input on not just the mayor and a replacement but the high school issue as well. Mom and Dad were always supportive of them all working together on things, and usually, they would come to a good conclusion about things long before the end of the meal. Fowler loved his family very much because they were good together.

~*~

Amy didn't want to have this meeting today. She had plenty to do that didn't involve her going to a meeting with a bunch of rich people that she didn't know. Of course, if they could help out with the school project, then she would put up with them. But she had a feeling that these people were used to getting their own way, and they weren't going to be very open-minded about the ideas that she had. She fucking hated rich people with a passion.

She was the first to arrive at the restaurant that they suggested. Again, it was a rich person place to eat that had things like wraps and small plates. She didn't go out enough to know what either meant, but she was in a pissy mood, so she didn't try to work out what she was going to be eating.

Picking out the most expensive place in town to tell her that they weren't going to do shit was the plan she'd bet. When her water was brought to her, she was told that the people she was meeting were running slightly behind and that they wanted her to order so it would be ready when they arrived.

"I'll just have a house salad." She was sure that she could afford that but wasn't positive. When the waiter winked at her, telling her that the Walshs would be picking up the tab, she told him that she just wanted the salad. "And don't make assumptions about me where you might get your ass handed to you."

"I'm profoundly sorry, miss." His face had turned a bright red, but she didn't feel the least bit guilty about putting him in his place. She wanted to get up and leave, but the family she was meeting with were coming toward her, and she lifted her chin when they asked her if she'd order.

"Yes. Now that you're all here, what are your plans for the school? I have things that I have to get to—"

"We never talk business until we've eaten. It's a hard and firm rule. And you can tone it down a bit. You're the one who had the idea that you meet with us, and we're here because of that." Amy decided that she could have hit the man in the face just to damage his good looks. "As I was saying, we never discuss business on an empty stomach. Have you decided to comply, or are we going to forgo the meal until later?"

She was embarrassed. She had been rude and snarky and didn't care for it when people were that to her. Telling them that she was sorry she was glad to see that their food was coming. Her salad and a thick burger with all the trimmings were sat down in front of her.

"I didn't order this." The man, she still didn't know his name, told her that he had. "I don't want it. I ordered a salad for a reason."

"Because you're on a diet? That can't be it. You're much too thin as it is. Because you were trying to make a point? I don't know what that would be because not getting a good meal isn't something that is a good idea for anyone. Eat the burger, and we'll talk." The woman with the man, his mother, she assumed, told him to behave himself. "I am. I've not force-fed her anything as yet. And you said yourself that she's much too thin as soon as we saw her. Not that it's any of our business, but I'd like to be able to look at myself in the mirror—"

"I bet you do that a great deal. Look at yourself in the mirror. You're just arrogant enough to know that you're very handsome and your being wealthy means that you get your own way about a great many things. Well, I'm not impressed with you. I'll eat what I want, and you'll just be happy that I don't shove this burger into your fucking face. You're a bully, and I would have hoped that your mother would have pointed that out to you."

"Now you listen here. I don't want to be here with you any more than you do. Especially since you decided to come here with a chip on your shoulder as big as a tree. You're nothing but a human, and I could have you for my dinner, but for the fact that you'd probably give me heartburn." She stood up when he did. "Eat."

"Fuck you." When she started to skirt around the table, he put his hand on her arm to no doubt stop her. But she wasn't going to stand for him manhandling her on top of everything else. Drawing back, she slammed her fist into his face hard enough that she knocked him back. Completely forgetting that he still held her, she landed atop him on the floor with a broken chair under them both.

Pain seared through her body when she started to move. Looking down her body to see if he'd hurt her, she saw the long, thin piece of wood sticking through her ribs. It was also protruding from him as well through his back into her. When he put his hands on her back to hold her still, she felt both dizzy and faint at the same time.

"Don't move. Please?" She nodded, sick now with the pain. "I'm going to...you're not going to like this any better than you do me, but I'm going to claim you right now. Just please, for the both of us to be able to heal from this, just tell me that you accept me. You're going to die if you don't."

"I'm sick." He nodded and told her that he knew, but she was going to have to accept him. "I don't know what that means. Accept you as what?"

"Mate." She knew the word and knew what it meant. Amy started to shake her head at him, but it was too much. Lying her head on his chest, the pain and loss of blood were making her weak. "Amy, I claim you as my mate. Will you accept me as such? You have to say the word. Please. You're running out of time. Your blood is flowing quickly, and you're going to die if you don't say you accept me."

"I'm hurting. Am I really going to die on top of you? I don't like you one bit." He told her that he wasn't all that thrilled either. "Great. All right. I guess that I accept you. Yes. I don't want to die. I don't want you either, but I don't want to die more."

Something stirred over her. She didn't know what it was, really she didn't care, but when she closed her eyes against the colors that were seemingly everywhere, she knew that she was dead and that her entire life would be nothing. She hadn't accomplished a single thing to make it so that people would remember her. Not even her family.

Amy wasn't sure that she'd ever known that death was so pretty. The things that she saw made her think that she'd been taken to another world in her repose. There were little people all over the place. Even whatever she was lying on was much more comfortable than any bed that she'd ever slept in.

The colors alone were enough to make her thrilled that she'd been killed. Earthtones, like she'd ever imagined before, seemed to be in every place that she looked. Even though she was dead and sorry about that, she was happy that her afterlife was so much nicer than her own place.

"Amy? Can you hear me?" She didn't want the asshole man to be there, so she turned away from his voice. "I need for you to move your arms for me. Just enough that I can make sure that your wound is healing properly."

"You just want me to die. Go away. I'm having

a good — are you dead too? And here to haunt me for the rest of my afterlife? If that's so, then you find yourself someplace and keep away from me. This is the best life I've had in forever." He told her that neither of them were dead but that he needed to check on her. "I am too dead. Nothing in life was ever this good. Go away and leave me alone. I don't want to be with you."

She didn't see him move, but he was suddenly gone. The next time she heard a voice, it was that of a woman. Amy didn't know who she was, but she seemed to be about as kind as the man was an asshole.

"He can be a pain in the ass when it suits him, I'll agree with you on that. You're almost well enough to wake now, Amy, my dear. If you would be so kind as to open your eyes, then you'll see that you're very much alive and doing well." She told the voice that she had been killed and it wasn't her fault. "No, it was neither of your faults that you came together in such a way. But it was imperative that you both live for all mankind. Open your eyes, Amy, my child. For it's time for you to begin your life with us."

She didn't see any reason to open her eyes, so she tightened them so that she'd not be tempted.

However, her curiosity got the better of her, and she opened them. Amy didn't move her body but her eyes. Even that proved to be exhausting for her, and she felt them drift closed again. When the woman insisted that she wake, it was all she could do not to scream at her to leave her alone. Her death, she told her, was so much better than the life she'd been living.

Amy realized as soon as she opened her eyes that she wasn't anywhere she'd been before. She also realized that she wasn't dead. That fact both depressed her and made her happy, too. Sitting up, she didn't feel any pain, but she was weak. Remembering what had happened to her, she laid back down and let the memory of being hurt so badly rush over her. When someone cleared their throat, she looked to see someone standing in the doorway with a book in her hand.

"We've never formally met. My name is Storm Walsh. I'm Mother to the arrogant asshole, as you call him, that you were hurt with." Amy asked her where she was. "At my home. Well, one of them. I don't care to be here overly much, but it was the only place to bring you so that you'd be able to heal. You have done well, much better than we thought you would, with the magic that you received. Would you like to get out of bed?"

"I don't know. Will I hurt if...you said one of your homes. Why do I have the feeling that this place isn't anything like any other house that I've been to." Storm came deeper into the room and sat down. "You're very beautiful. Also, you look like you're glowing. That could be just me, but I'm sure that there is something that you're not telling me. A lot as a matter of fact."

"And you'd be correct. I will tell you, but I'm not the sort of person that fucks around with telling people shit. Do you want it nice and slow or all at once? I can give it to you as you can tolerate it, but I don't think you're going to be any less upset about how it turned out." She told her to tell her where she was. "All right. You're in my castle. Before it was mine, it was my mother's. You've spoken to her. Several times while you were resting. This castle is the one for the dragon queen. Okay, so far?"

"There is no such thing as dragons." Storm only smiled. "All right. You seem to be sane, so let's just say that there are dragons and that you're one. Why am I in your castle?"

"When the two of you were impaled on the

wood, you were as close to death as any human that I've ever encountered. But when my son, Fowler, you didn't seem to know his name when you were out, he claimed you; he was doing so to save you. Not that he's any more thrilled about you being his mate than you seemed to have been, but both your lives were spared. You're now immortal, as are all of us." Amy nodded but didn't say anything. "Do you have questions for me?"

"Plenty, but I don't know that I have the head to ask them in any kind of order right now. So his claiming me? It saved my life. I had a feeling that he kind of wished me dead." She only shrugged. "I'm going to ignore the fact that you didn't agree or disagree with me. Okay, so dragon again. You really think that you're a dragon. Not only that, but it is something akin to being their boss. Right?"

"Yes. I'm their queen. My mom was a queen before me, but she decided to retire, and I took her place. I wasn't all that happy about it, but there was no choice for me to take the position, so I stepped up. Mom, her name is Morning, wanted to see more of the world that she helped to create and save, and I, and my husband, my mate, Alex, took over. I have to admit it's been a good deal more fun than I thought it would be. You'll meet Alex later. He's working on some projects for me." She asked her if Alex was a dragon. "No, well, he was a vampire of considerable age when I met him. However, when I claimed him, he became more than that."

"Right. A vampire. You do know that people don't believe in them either." She told her that was the reason that he was able to live for so long." Getting up, she felt better. Moving around, it made her feel better still. She realized that she was thirsty. More than that, she was starving as well. "Do you have a kitchen here? Where they might serve something more than…what do you eat anyway? Do they bring, I don't know, cows around for you to devour?"

"You don't need to be snarky, Amy. That's my job." Telling her she was sorry but overwhelmed. "Yes, you are, but you're snarky as well. Come with me. We have a well-stocked pantry here that will meet your needs for food. And in answer to your question, yes, we eat regular food like you do. Only as our dragons do we partake of cows and the like."

She wasn't sure what to believe anymore. Then she entered the kitchen. Amy stood there, knowing that her mouth was wide open, staring at what could only be described as a magical dwelling. And boy, oh boy, was it magical.

Chapter 2

Fowler was going over the seams of the timelines he'd been asked to go over an hour ago. Sometimes, even with the computers helping them with the timelines, there were small mistakes, little places where the time would be wrong. Nothing that he couldn't fix, but he had too much on his mind to worry over if the little kitten that had moved when it shouldn't have was in two places at the same time. But he did fix it. He knew that someone somewhere would find it and complain. Just as he was putting the timeline in the right place, he felt a presence that he'd not felt in this room before.

"What do you want?" Amy wasn't doing anything but standing in the doorway to his office. She'd not even said a word, not a sound that would make him feel any less pissed off than he was. When she didn't answer him, he asked her again what she wanted.

"Your mother sent me here. And in her sending me here, I mean I just appeared here instead of going home as I had suggested that I wanted to do. Why are you forever in a shitty mood? I mean, I would have thought that it was me, but I've not been around you for hours, so that can't be it. However, I have heard from your brothers that you've been in this mood for decades. I can see that, too." He said that it was her presence that put him there. "As I said, I wasn't here, so that can't be it. I'm to come here and ask you if you would enjoy having dinner with your grandmother and parents. I haven't any idea why I should be the one asking you when you have a link to your parents and grandmother as well as your brothers. Why are they trying to push us together? I think we've made it—"

"Do you forever empty your head? Spewing out shit that no one gives a crap about? I don't like it, so stop it right now." He put the timeline away and turned back to the door. She was gone. While he knew that he could find her, it was the fact that he had to go looking for her to see why she'd left the area.

It took him nearly three hours to figure out that

Amy wasn't in the building he was in. It might well have taken him less time had he thought about what he was doing, finding places where she'd been and enjoying her scent as it lingered behind her. But she was no more in the building than his parents were. Christ. Now, he was going to have to tell his parents that he'd lost Amy when they'd sent her to him.

Since he had very little to no information about Amy before he'd claimed her, he didn't know where he might have to look to see if she had gone home. Wherever home was. She was more than likely there plotting his demise, he thought. It would be just like the fates, he supposed to put him with someone who didn't listen and had homicidal tendencies on top of being an irritant. When he showed up at his mom's home, she met him at the door with a look on her face that told him that he'd fucked up badly.

"When I send someone to ask you a question, Fowler, you're not to make them feel like shit because you're in a shitty mood. What the hell is wrong with you all the time? Do you like having me pissed off at you? I'm thinking that you do. And I'm frankly sick of having to apologize to people that you've been rude to." He said that he didn't ever want her pissed off at him. But that he didn't want a mate either.

"Then why did you claim her?"

He stared at his mother for several seconds. "She would have died. Don't you remember that? You were right there. Is that what you wanted me to do? Let her die?" She told him it would have been better had he done that than to kill her daily with his words. "I'm not killing her with my words. If she's going to be around me, she's going to have to get used to the way I am. I didn't ask for her to be my mate."

She didn't move when he took a step to enter the house. But when he moved to go around her, she blocked his passage. He asked her if he was being barred from her home.

"Yes." He stood there, thinking that this couldn't be right. That somehow Amy had turned his mother—the slap to his face hurt. More because his mother had done it. "Go away, Fowler. Just leave here while I still love you. Right now, all I can think about is the fact that you're blaming a child that had no more to do with you being her mate than your father was mine. At least I accepted him. You keep pushing her away. She told me that she wished that she'd never said those words to you that made her your mate. That she, too, wished that she'd died that day." Figures. No one appreciated the sacrifices that he had given up when taking her that day.

"I did it because she would have died. Is that what you would have wanted?" She just turned on her heel and left him standing there. "You didn't answer me."

When his dad came to the doorway, he asked him if he was to block him from coming in. Instead of answering him, he moved to the swing on the porch and sat down. He wasn't sure if he was to join him or not, so he stood there as his dad began to speak.

"Amy has decided to take a job that will take her far from here. I'm helping her out by providing her with transportation and gear." He asked his dad if he was doing this to piss him off. "Believe it or not, Fowler, the world does not revolve around you. She's a nice person. And when you ever get your head out of your ass and realize that, you could have a good life. But I'm not going to have her suffer at your hand any longer. Mostly your mouth. You're caustic and tearing at her in ways that won't heal if you keep this up. She's hurting deep within her heart, and it's all because of you."

"So this is my fault." His dad only looked at him. "I don't know what it is that I've done. I've kept her from dying, and now I'm the bad guy. You and Mom seem to think that she would have been better off letting her die than to make it so that she'll live forever."

"She might well have been better off." He didn't know what to say, so he didn't open his mouth. Dad had never been one to mince words, neither had his mom. But right now, he wished they'd just tell him what they wanted of him and be done with it. He'd rather be mated to Amy than to have his parents at odds with him. He asked his dad when Amy was leaving. "She left today. And don't ask me where she is. I won't tell you. If you wish to talk to her, as a civilized person, then it will be on your own to find her. I'm finished with you and her being what could be the best thing that has ever happened to you."

"So everyone is pissed off at me because of her." Dad just laughed. "You know, I don't know what it is that I'm supposed to do? Fuck her until she's has my kid? Then what will that—" His dad just disappeared.

He could do that, thanks to his magic as an old vampire, but it made him no less startled by it. Dad had only done that to him once before. And then they'd been arguing too. Fowler didn't like arguing with his family. Especially over something so stupid as a woman. And as far as he was concerned, this was by far the stupidest woman he'd ever encountered. And now, because of her, he was at odds with not just his father but most of his family as well.

In one month, she'd turned his entire family against him. Getting up, he decided to go home and just stay there. If they didn't want him around, then he'd just not be around. As he made his way to his car, he decided that he was going to take a vacation. He didn't even care where he went. He was just going to go and not tell anyone where he was. That would serve them right, he figured. Fowler could cut them out of his life as easily as they had cut him out of theirs. He didn't care either that he was sounding childish. This was all on Amy.

Instead, as soon as he got home, he realized that he had too much unfinished work on his desk to enjoy any kind of vacation. Putting things in order of importance, even putting the school project at the top of the list, he began sorting through all the things that he'd been putting off since meeting and claiming Amy. Almost as soon as he began reading over some of the other projects he'd been putting off, Fowler realized that it had been a good while since he'd sat down at his desk. Some of the projects that he'd been putting off were as much as a decade old. He started on those first.

By the time he was getting started with only the first four things on his list, he was having fun. It had always been a blast for him to get projects started and underway. Not only had he a crew of faeries working on the new building for the school, but he also had some of the younger dragons clearing the way for the parking lot that would hold a great many more cars than the previous lot had.

The second thing on his list was what to do with the old school. Several projects could use the old building, but he realized after having a look at what needed to be done to bring it up to code that it would cost much more than it would just to tear it down and start over. As it was now, there were thousands of dollars going into the building monthly just to keep the heat on. There wasn't any cooling in the building at all, and it made it unbearable, he'd bet, to be in the classrooms in the summer months. Then there were the bathrooms, flooring, as well as the furnace, plumbing, and internet that needed to be upgraded.

He worked the rest of the afternoon and well

into the night. Lunch was brought to him at some point, he realized, and the dish or dishes had been taken away just as quietly. There were crumbs all over the corner of his desk, and somehow, he'd gotten mustard on his tie. He didn't like to be bothered when he was working. It would interrupt his flow of thoughts, and he needed that when he was working on several projects at the same time.

By nearly sunrise again, he was putting the last of his work in neat piles, each in a file folder that he could easily pull up when talking about the things going on with them. Fowler was proud of himself. He'd not gotten distracted once, and he was able to keep his family from coming over and brow-beating him for answers about Amy.

Stretching his large frame, he made his way to his bedroom. He was going to have to get himself a home soon. Living in an apartment limited him in doing things like having his own yard. Even if he didn't want Amy around to bug the shit out of him, she'd need a large place to live. It occurred to him as he was pulling the blankets off the bed that he didn't have the slightest idea where she was staying, nor for that matter, what her full name was. He'd have to have one of his brothers look into that for him so that he could put her name on a couple of credit cards.

But she wasn't going to make him broke. He would limit her spending and make sure that when he wanted his money, it would be right where he wanted it. He knew women like Amy. Thinking that they had an endless supply of money simply because he did. Well, that shit wasn't going to be happening to him.

Lying his head down on his pillow, he thought of something else that he'd put off about her. She was going to need to be groomed on how to act properly when he had guests around. And while he didn't entertain a great deal, there were times when he'd have to be present with a woman on his arm to make sure that the family was well thought of and well represented at all times. He wasn't going to be escorting around a harpy that would embarrass not just him but his family as well.

Fowler had never had any trouble falling asleep in all his life. Tonight, with his mind nagging at him about Amy and what she might be up to had him tossing and turning for so long that he finally gave up getting any kind of rest and made his way to the shower.

He might as well get a good start on the things

that he'd lined up and stop letting things pile up on his desk. Also, he was going to call a realtor to find him a home that he could live in that would offer the most distance between him and his new mate. Things, he thought were starting to look better when he made some decisions regarding Amy that would give her what her parents wanted, a safe home, but also kept her out of his life as much as possible.

He wasn't even going to think about having any kind of sexual relationship with her. Not yet, anyway. She had a lot of training to go through, and he wasn't going to be sucked into her life because she had a pretty face and body.

By the time he was ready to meet with his brother Melbourne, he had a comprehensive list of things that he could get started on before they had to approach the county about the new school. It was going to cost a good deal more to put the place in town where the other had been because of the sheer amount of land that would be required to build it. He had taken Amy's suggestion and did add double the parking space into the land, but there were going to be a great many houses as well as the demolition of some prime land that might be better served in bringing in some businesses. Melbourne agreed with him. To a point.

"I don't like that we're tearing down the old building for no other reason than it needs to be down." He grinned at him. Melbourne hadn't heard, he thought, what a supposed prick he'd been to his mate. "That didn't come out right. What I mean is, while we have the construction equipment there, can we do something that will at least make it look like we're working toward something and not just going to have a dirty area for the kids to get into trouble with."

"What do you have in mind?" They tossed around a couple of ideas, but the one that Madison liked when he joined them in the discussion was the new stadium and parking. "You think that the town will go for that?"

"I don't know why not. The team went all the way to state last year and the year before. We should reward them for their hard work. I know you didn't play that much football, but I remember that field. It was hard and dry most of the summer and when fall rolled around, the thing was so full of holes full of water that you'd nearly break your leg just running laps."

Sidney and Edgar joined them when they

stopped by the Dari-twist to get lunch. Edgar had played football, and he had more stories to tell about the field than they had wanted. Also, the seating. They were still using concrete seats that were so crumbly and dangerous that he knew a kid had gotten hurt last year when he'd been cheering on his brother.

"Where's Amy?" No one moved when Sidney asked him where she was. It wasn't until Madison threw a French fry at him that he felt his temper rise up. "Is it true that you don't want her around, Fowler, and only accepted her so that she'd not die? That can't be right. Not even for you."

"Why not? Do you think that I should have taken her to my place and let her have free reign over my life? Spend all my money and leave me a broken—where are you going?" Madison said he had better things to do today as he and the others began getting up and leaving him there. "Because you don't agree with my views?"

"No one agrees with your views. But I'm staying out of it. Right up until she comes to me on how to remove your head from your body and—do you not know where she is, Fowler? Do you even care?" He said that so long as she wasn't nipping at his heels in him giving her his money, he didn't care. "Anyone of us have enough money right now that we could easily afford to give every person in his town a million dollars, and it wouldn't hurt us a bit. How much do you think she's going to want from you? Christ, Dad was right. You're a bitter old man that has his entire life right in front of him, but he can't see it for the shit that you've thought up in your head."

They left him there, like they arrived, leaving him one at a time. Sidney was the last to leave, and he asked him if he wanted to be seen with him. That's when he realized that he had gone too far with his little brother. The shot to his face, his fist slamming hard into his nose and mouth, knocked him back off the bench they'd been on and into the little wooded area behind him. Then he got up and walked away without another word. He wanted to blame that on Amy as well, but he'd been fighting with his brothers for the last decade or so, and it was getting worse all the time.

~*~

Amy loved Texas. Well, not the heat, but she did enjoy the food and the people. They seemed to be having as much fun as she had when she had visited their vendor stalls around the oceanfront. Who knew that there would be such a variety of food and people in the same country that she had grown up in.

But she thought that she was enjoying the camping the best. When Alex told her that he'd help her get away from Fowler so he could cool off, Amy didn't think there was a place far enough or deep enough that she could hide in. The younger man's temper seemed to be off the charts all the time, especially around her. However, when he suggested for her to come here to check out the area for a project that he was working on, she took him up on the deal.

Amy had thought that it was just a way for her to be forgotten about. To send her off on a wild goose chase while the rest of them had a good laugh about how she'd been fooled into thinking they were all dragons. But she'd been so very wrong about a great many things about the Walsh family.

Foremost, they were dragons. She'd not seen one of them as yet, but when she'd been recuperating, she'd spent some time outside the room she'd been in. The first several days had been quiet, nothing out of the ordinary going on. The trees did seem to be brighter and the air cleaner, but there wasn't anything that made her think that she had fallen over the—not even the little people in the kitchen had seemed as real as they did there in the land of color and magic.

Amy had seen not just several dragons that were lounging around in the yard and flying high in the sky, but around the honest-to-goodness castle, she'd seen unicorns, trolls, and a whole colorful array of the pretties little creatures that she'd ever imagined in her life. Little tiny people with bright wings and sparkly hair. And they spoke to her. Every time she was out there with them, they told her stories about the life they lived. What they'd done that day and named the flowers that she couldn't have recalled if her life depended on it.

"Lady Amy, did you know that no one here will take you to task about practicing your magic." She didn't bother telling the little man that she didn't have magic. She had a lot of it, she thought, for someone just being a human. However, she didn't call herself human anymore, either. They were very vocal about her being the queen of all dragons someday. "You should see what else you can do with what you received from Lord Fowler."

Amy didn't say anything negative about Lord Fowler. Never once did she complain about the fact that he had sent her away so that he'd not be bothered with her. His dad had told her what Fowler had been thinking and wanting from her. It hurt her to her core that Lord Fowler had been so cruel to her when she'd never said or done anything that would warrant such a response from him. Amy wasn't all that thrilled about being mated to him, either. And she was happy to be here, with the little people that had come with her to hide away from him.

While she was thinking about the few things that she had figured out, nothing earth-shattering like she had imagined, she looked down at the little fire that she had in front of her and saw something shining brightly against the red flames of heat.

Before she could even think what she was doing, Amy reached into the flame and pulled out the little orb. But she was distracted by what happened to her when she fisted the orb. Her hand was on fire. The flames that had been in the wood that she'd been heating water with had heated up her hand. Almost as soon as she realized that she was on fire, she patted her hand on her clothing to put out the flames as they ran not just up her fingers but to her elbow as well.

"Are you injured, my lady?" She nodded, then realized that she wasn't hurt and shook her head. Lifting her hand up, she could see that there were no blisters on her finger, nothing that looked like she'd just burnt herself. Even her clothing which she'd been sure had caught fire, was perfectly fine without a single mark on them. "My lady?"

"It didn't hurt. I mean, It should have. Badly, but it didn't hurt me." She ran her fingers over the flames again, realizing that it really didn't hurt her at all. "It's like it has no effect on me whatsoever."

When she looked at Donka, her faerie, she realized that his face was telling her that she shouldn't be handling her hand's ability to catch on fire well. Putting both of her hands under her legs, she told the little man that she was fine now that she must have been mistaken about touching it. He nodded but didn't say anything else as the two of them sat there staring at anything but the fire or each other.

"Did you get what you found?" It took her befuddled mind a few seconds to remember the orb she'd seen in the flames. Finding it again, this time in the dirt, she picked it up and shoved it into her pocket, telling Donka that she would toss it out later. Everything about the evening was ruined, she thought, simply because she'd been able to—"King Alex sent you some cash. I hadn't realized that you would need anything being so far from his lordship. He said that you are to use it on whatever you fancy and that he would expect you to show him all the treasures that you find while here in Tex-ass." They all called the state that. Like it really was Tex with an ass on the end.

"I'll do that." Glancing in the direction of the camper that had been provided for her when she arrived here, Amy knew that she'd never spend the money that was provided for anything other than food or necessities. As soon as she was able to work a few more weeks for the pizza place, she'd have enough of her own money to be able to travel farther away from the Walsh family. Not just them but one in particular. It was nearing midnight when she finally put out her little fire and made her way to the camper. Telling Donka good night, she wasn't the least bit surprised to watch him sit on the step of the camper where she would find him the next morning.

Settling on the bed, not touching anything other than what she needed, Amy looked around the spacious room. It was larger than her apartment was, with just this single room. The bathroom, one on each end of the thing, was nice. The bathtub was big enough for her to lay out flat in it and not be crowded or cramped. She'd not had a bath in it yet. She wouldn't either. Instead, she was using the bathroom shower in the gas station across the street from where she was staying. The Walsh family would want to resell the camper, and she was going to make it look as nice as the day that it was shown to her when she arrived. Pulling out the journal that she'd been reading since arriving, Amy laid down on the bed and opened the book.

After receiving the book from Fowler's grandmother a few days after she was able to get up and around, she couldn't read the floral handwriting that was on each page. Now, for some reason, not only could she read the book, but she understood some of the text that she was sure was above her head. Not that she thought she was stupid, but it had been in dragon, a language that she hadn't learned. Donka told her that it was because the queen had given her the abilities so that she'd understand what it was like to be a mate to a great dragon. She snorted at that reason again, the same as she had the first time.

Now that she was more than halfway through the book, she understood more about the creature Grail, too, that everyone was looking for. The man who was willing to kill off all dragons, thus the faeries, and other small creatures as well to make himself king. After reading the chapter about what would happen to the world without the magic that the dragons provided, it took her several days to realize that Fowler would be necessary to keep up the continuation of magic as well. He would, according to the book, be king someday, and he'd rule the lands as needed.

She wondered how that would piss him off but read the next lines in the book instead of getting into that again. But all her mind wanted to do was to go back out in the area she'd been staying and try and see what else she could do with the fire. So far, the only thing that Amy had been able to find out about the use of fire was that there had once been a flame starter.

It was never clear in the book if the Starter was a male or female. It had been clear, however, that the Starter had gone to each new hatchling dragon born when it was of a certain age and given them the breath of flames. It was a powerful job, and Starter was very kind and good at making sure that the right flames went to the right dragon. Amy had already figured out that there were hundreds of kinds of dragons around and as many flames to go with them.

However, when the hatchlings began to be less and less, she surmised that it was her kind that had done that to them. The Starter's job became boring to her. So one day, after going to the queen and king, the Starter decided that the parent of the hatchling would know best what flame was needed for their own child. After teaching each family of dragons the way to use the flame starter and the knowledge of how to make it work, the Starter simply disappeared.

It was well past midnight when she put the book away for the night. She hated to do that. Each page of the book was like a new adventure to her. Amy didn't know what she was going to do when she was finished with the book. Hopefully, there were others that she could read and let her imagination run wild with the thoughts of flying high in the sky as a big dragon and having the power to do whatever she wanted to make the world a better place.

At three o'clock the next afternoon, after playing with the flames and making her own discoveries, she felt a pain so deep in her body that she was sure that she was going to bleed to death before finding the source. The thought of stepping into the flame and it taking her to Fowler, who she only just realized was the one hurt. Amy appeared in the flames next to the bloodied body of Fowler and a man standing over him laughing.

Chapter 3

Opening his eyes, Fowler didn't move. He knew where he was and knew that, on some level, whatever had happened to bring him to his grandmother's castle had been terrible. Moving his hand up to touch his throat, he heard his dad laughing. Then Amy.

"You cheated." Chess. He had no idea why he knew that Amy and his dad were playing chess, but his dad was a terrible player, and in order to make himself feel better about losing every time, he would accuse, jokingly, that the other person was cheating. Amy told his dad that she didn't cheat and then asked him if he was allowing her to win. "Yes. That's it. I'm allowing you to win to make you look better. Not that you need all that much help to look beautiful, but I'm going to stick with that. Would you like another game?"

"Your son is awake, and I must leave. I have

things that need my attention, Lord Alex." He scolded
her for calling him that, but she stood. He could just
make out her face when she disappeared. Careful of
sitting up, he asked his dad if she was all right.

"She is. Better than you were. But you're
healing, and that's the important thing." Fowler told
his dad that he didn't remember anything. "You will
soon enough. You can have some soft foods for now.
Soup and some greens but nothing more. I was told
that you couldn't have anything too cold or hot, and
I'm holding you to that."

Dad helped him set up more in the bed by
putting extra pillows behind him. Feeling better in
small doses, Fowler asked his dad where Amy had
gone.

"She doesn't tell any of us much of anything.
She just comes and goes when she wishes none of us
would try to stop her or ask questions. I don't know
how much you're going to remember, but she made
sure that we were called in to bring you here so
that you'd —" Dad got up and went to the window.
"None of us know what happened that day. Grail
was there. We've surmised that much. And he tried
to kill you. Other than that, his death, Grails, I mean,
is something that none of us have been able to piece

together."

"Amy was there. I remember seeing her." Dad nodded. "Grail. I remember now. He came at me from behind and sliced—"

Fowler remembered the pain of his head being taken from his shoulders. The laughter of Grail as he stood over him. There was more, but his mind was too focused on the fact that he was here and his head had been removed. The only way to kill him was to remove his head from his shoulders.

The pain to his face had him looking at his father. He was telling him to breathe and that everything was all right. Twice more, he slapped him when he just couldn't bring enough air into his lungs. But it was the fear that tightened around him that he just couldn't shake that easily.

"He didn't succeed. It was close. The physician at the castle said that it was a mere inch that still connected your head to your throat. Nothing more than a small flap of skin that kept you from dying right then." He said that he remembered flames, too, and Grail screaming in pain. "We knew nothing of that. Amy…she's not telling us anything. I'm sure that she knows just what happened, but—"

"Bring her here, and I'll make her tell us." Dad

turned to look at him, and it hurt Fowler to his heart that his dad was disappointed in him. Before he could speak again, not even sure what he'd say to him, Dad turned his back to him and spoke without looking at him.

"She came here right away after you were brought here. Amy has the traits of a vampire as old, if not older than I am. She gave you, willingly and without anyone asking her to do it, much too much of her blood to keep you from dying. It was so powerful, son, that your neck healed immediately and without any scarring." He wondered what she would want in return for that, but as soon as the thought went through his mind, he knew that she'd want nothing. She could have easily let him die out there, severing the last bit of flesh on his neck to end him. "There are other things too that she can do. Some I have witnessed on my own, but others I have gotten little glimpse of when she is here with me and you. She hasn't left your side since…well, it matters little to you, I suppose. She came here to save your life, and she did."

"Dad, I'm sorry. So sorry." His dad told him that he was saying that to the wrong person. "I think that I've really fucked up. What I've been doing…it's running around in my head, and I believe that I've really fucked up any kind of relationship that I could have had...hopefully will have with Amy."

"You have." The burst of laughter startled him. Fowler couldn't remember the last time that he'd found enjoyment out of anything. "She's a wonderful person. Giving so generously of her heart and mind. Speaking of which, Amy read the book that your grandmother gave you. There are a lot of things that she knows that none of us did. Not even your grandmother. However, I fear that now that you're awake and talking, she'll take off again. I don't know...not with the power she has that we'll be able to find her again."

Anger surged through him again, and he nearly lashed out at his dad to make Amy stay with them—for him when he knew that would be the end of everything. Instead, Fowler took in several deep breaths and let them out slowly. On some level, he knew that he shouldn't be so obvious about holding his temper, but it had been forever since he'd even tried to curb his annoyance or shut his mouth. When Fowler looked at his dad, he could see the look on his face that he'd put there. Disappointment. So much of it that he put his hand over his heart to help with the sudden pain there.

"I'm going to need some help." Dad asked him for what. "With Amy." He thought about that for a second. "That's not what I meant to say, but I want help with Amy so that she might like me — all I can ever hope for at this point in our lives, don't you think? No, don't answer that. I need hope. And just today, I find that I want her to be in my life. It probably has more to do with me — Sorry excuse as well. I nearly died, and I just realized that I don't want to, and I want to have the next forever years spending them getting to know her."

"She's not going to be nice to you. Not that I blame her for not wanting to be with you. I don't know where you — well, I have an idea that you got your thoughts on how to treat women from your great-grandmother. Tisha, the fucking bitch. Someday, and I have a feeling that she's going to be coming around sooner rather than later when she finds out you have a mate. Watch…" Dad laughed. "I was going to tell you to watch out for Amy when she comes around, but I think that it would be more fun to watch the two of them tangle. Tisha will try to make her listen to what she says, but I don't think Amy will do that anymore than she's been listening to you."

When his dad left him, Fowler went back to the bed he'd been when he woke. There were things that were running through his mind that he didn't want to dwell on, so he got up and took a shower. Even there, when he'd been washing his neck, his mind turned the flowing warm water into hot blood running out of his—"

"What the fuck is w—You're hyperventilating, dumbass. Breathe. In and out. You haven't forgotten how to do that, have you?" He was hyperventilating, and he couldn't seem to get it under control. The slap to his face startled him enough that not only did he stop breathing, but he nearly slipped on the tile floor to get away from whoever hit him. "Do I need to hit you again? Fucking breathe before I have to punch you this time."

All at once, his breathing started again. It also caused him to inhale sharply, which, again, made him think of blood, his blood as it ran from his throat to the ground he'd fallen to. Reaching out blindly, Fowler thought that it was Amy the way she was berating him, but he wasn't that sure. He pulled whoever it was to him.

"Breathe. I've got you. Just breathe." He did, taking in huge gulps of air and coughing it out just as quickly. "Damn it, Fowler, if this is your plan to get me naked with you, I'm going to—" His mind was back there, back to the night he'd been nearly killed.

"He cut my throat. I was just sitting there when I felt the faint air as it stirred around my neck. My first thought was that I'd been brushed by a small branch from the tree above me. Then the pain, very little at first, then more as my head began to slip forward off my— Blood. There was blood all over me, and I knew that I was going to die." Fowler pulled back but didn't loosen his tight grip on Amy. He was terrified. "I saw you there then. You were fire. Not on fire but you were the fire that I'd lit earlier that evening. My mind didn't want to work that out until I saw you reaching beyond the fire that covered you and wrapped your hands around his throat. Grail, he screamed. Screamed and screamed over and over until his head just wasn't there any longer." He pulled her into his arms, forgetting everything but what he'd seen that night. "You put my head back to my shoulders, I think. I could only see the darkness, and right now, I'm thinking that I could smell the earth and blood then. I felt my hair being pulled, set right, I guess. I could see the fire and your feet."

"I had just read that day that dragons could only

be killed one of two ways. The first one makes perfect sense when you think about it and leads right into the second one. When falling from a great distance and landing on their head is first. The second is to have the dragon's head removed. It is said completely in its own sentence. Remove a dragon's head, period then, completely with a period at the end of that. Like they needed to make sure — anyway. I pushed your head into position so that the healing process could start. That's all there is to it. Just have the head moved so that it will fully attach itself to the neck and shoulders."

"What would have happened had there been nothing left? No attachment at all to my neck?" Amy simply looked him in the eye and told him that he'd of been as dead as Grail. "You saved my life."

"I did." Detaching herself from him, she dragged one of the super large towels to her and tossed it in his direction. "You need to get dressed. Your grandmother is demanding that I go to her estate and answer questions about Grail. If you can confirm for her that I didn't cut you in the first place, I'd appreciate it very much."

"I can do that." She was distancing herself from him. Not that he thought that they'd ever been close, but she didn't want to be around him, and all for good reasons, too. "Is there a dress code? Or can I go like I am, minus being soaking wet?"

He looked at her then. Really looked and realized that he'd never done that before. Fowler had had an idea that she was beautiful. But she was so much more than that.

Dark hair and even darker colored eyes. When she turned to look at him again, he could see that they weren't dark blue but the most beautiful purple he'd ever seen. Much darker than the purple amethysts that he'd seen on the castle lands. And there was a spark in them that he was sure the spark was very telling in her nature.

"What are you looking at?" He told her that he was looking at her. A beautiful creature. "Well, I might well be something that you're going to want to destroy if this shit that I got from you claiming me gets any weirder. I can do things like a vampire that not even your dad can do. But we'll discuss that later. I'm being hammered into making you hurry so that we can get this shit over with about that guy's death." She reminded him about the dress code.

"No. I mean, I'd not go there in a swimsuit, but your shorts and shirt are fine. I'll wear the same if it'll make you feel better." Amy asked him why he'd care about her feelings on anything. "I deserve that. More if you're dishing out insults. I'd like to start over with you. I want...I don't know what I want from you, but I will tell you that I'll be thrilled with whatever you're willing to give me."

"Did your family tell you to do that since I saved your life?" He said that no one had said anything to him other than they were disappointed in him for his treatment of her. "Yeah? I'm disappointed, too, but that's on me. I found out, quite by accident, the other day that you're stupid wealthy." He asked her what that meant. "You can be stupid with your money, and no one will care because you have a seemingly endless supply of it."

He didn't mention that he did have an endless supply because all the rumors about dragon crying tears that turned to gems were true. Also, his family had been around so long that they had money from long-term investments and —

"Are you calculating how much you have?" He told her what he'd been thinking. "Yeah, stupid wealthy. You should move on without me. Nothing will happen to you. I mean, unlike vampires and other shifters, you could care less — which I've always

assumed that you didn't care if I was in your life or
not."

"I've had a near-death experience, and I've
changed my mind about a great many things. Like
I said before, I want us to start over." He put out his
hand and waited for her to make the first move. It
did bother him a little that she took so long to take
his hand, but when she did, the breath that he'd
been holding waiting on her seemed to come from
the bottom of his feet. "All right. Let's get going to
Grandmother's home and find out what is going on."

They arrived just as his mom was going toe to
toe with her grandmother. He'd been warned that
she might show up. He just wished he'd had longer
so that he could warn Amy about her. Not so much
warn her but give her a heads up that she would be
a royal bitch, something he was just beginning to
realize to anyone and everyone. When Amy put her
fingers in her mouth and let go of a shrill whistle. He
had to laugh. He'd never in his life seen his great-
grandmother speechless.

"What the fuck are you going on about?"
Grannie, what he decided to call his great-
grandmother from now on, looked at him when Amy
demanded that she answer the question. "I don't

have time for whatever you have going on in your head. I came here to answer some questions, and then we're leaving to work out some family issues."

"What do you mean to talk to me that way?" Amy told Grannie that she would speak to her just as she was speaking to everyone else. "I could have you killed right now."

With a snap of Grannie's fingers, the room filled with warrior faerie. Thousands upon thousands of them. And all their arrows, no doubt dipped in some kind of poison, pointed directly at Amy. When he started forward to, well, he didn't know what he might have done. He stopped when Amy put her hand up. Then, she addressed the horde.

"Even if one arrow leaves your bow, I don't care why. I will destroy the lot of you. Put your weaponry away, or there will be a lot of mourning by your families that you're going to leave behind." She made a small ball of fire in her hand and held it up to them. "There will be nothing left of you if I want. Nothing for a grave to put you in. Just dust. Are you willing to die for this woman who has no authority whatsoever?"

"She's our former queen." Amy pointed out that it would matter little to her if they died or not.

"She is our queen, my lady. We cannot go against her in any way."

"So you believe that she'll have a change of heart if she has one, and mourn your passing? That isn't going to happen. She'll just call in more of your kind in waves until every one of you are dead. Also, I want you to remember something as you decide if you want to live or die: I will be your future queen if it comes to that, and your answer, whether it's to die or not, will be remembered by the two of us for all time." Grannie looked at him, and he smiled. He thought that was very telling in how surprised she was that he'd found this particular woman to be his mate. And Fowler couldn't have been more proud of anyone than he was at that moment of his mate. "You have until the count of three."

Amy didn't get any further than three when they dropped their weapons and flew to the ceiling. Grannie, as pissed as he'd ever seen her stomped her way to Amy and got within inches of her when Amy smiled. Grannie stopped moving and stood there like she had plenty to say, but the words or whatever she'd been about to say were cut off.

"I can easily take you out, too." It wasn't a threat, he realized, when his grannie took a step backwards, but a promise. Amy made it in a clear, calm voice, but there was never any doubt in his mind that she would do it if his grannie made a single misstep and put her hands or used magic on Amy. "I'm not a person that you want to fuck with. I will gladly reach down into your throat and pull out what surely must be a stone as your heart and beat you to death with it."

Grannie backed up one step more. Then another. It wasn't long before she was at least several feet from Amy. Walking up behind her, telling Amy he was there before putting his hands on her shoulders, he kissed her throat and felt the shiver that went through her body.

Turning to his grandmother, he called out to her twice before she turned and looked at him. He didn't dare laugh, not at the expression on her face nor his attempts to get her attention. Tensions were riding a little too high for him to think that he might be hurt if anyone farted right now.

"You had some questions for Amy." She didn't speak but nodded. Then Grandmother shook herself slightly and smiled. Smiling back, he asked his grandmother again if she had questions. "We are going to work on our being a couple, and I'd like to get back to it if you'd not mind."

"No. I mean, yes, of course. I just..." Grandmother looked at him and then his dad before shaking her head and turning to look at Amy again. Her smile was brighter than before. "Since you're not a dragon, I don't think you are at any rate. I need to put to the record that you killed Grail. And whatever other information you might have about the night Fowler was hurt."

The book appeared on the table beside his grandmother and opened up on its own. Stepping closer, having had the book but he'd not read it, he was surprised to see that it was written in dragon. Snorting a little when he'd been taken off guard by the fact that Amy had read it in his own language didn't even make a blip on his mind to think how much she'd gotten from their one encounter that being at the restaurant. He wondered, scarily so, what they'd share if they made love.

After telling everyone in the room, including his brothers, parents, and his grannie, what had happened and how she'd come to be with him by jumping to him from one fire to the next.

"I don't believe you. It's doubtful that anyone would believe someone like her. Just look." Both he and Amy ignored Grannie. "She's gotten some of that disgusting vampire blood in her from that man over there. So we're all supposed to believe that she killed a being, a dragon being that was much stronger than anyone in this room. I say she tried to kill Fowler and then covered it up by killing some being and claimed that it was him who had done it. None of us should be believing a word that spews from her mouth."

"I saw her there." Grannie snorted. "I could care less what you believe right now and perhaps in my future dealings with you. But she was there, and it happened just as she said. She came out of the flames and burnt Grail to death. Then she saved my life. She, my mate, is the only reason that I'm where—I still have nightmares thinking about how so very easily I was nearly killed." Fowler let enough of his dragon go so that he knew how menacing he looked before he spoke again. "You talk about my father like that again, and you won't have to worry about whether or not Amy is strong enough to take you on. I know for a fact that I'm more than capable."

"I'll be there too." After Dyson spoke, stepping up behind him as he did, each of his brothers did the same. "There will be nothing left of you but flakes that no one will take a single pause for. I've had just about enough of your ways and insults."

Dad came to stand with him and the others and put his arm around them all for a group hug. Fowler, like a lot of things he was beginning to realize, had been missing a lot in the last several hundred years. He vowed to do it more often. Not just to hug but to do it to all his family members.

"Can you show us how you did that? I don't want you to think that I don't believe you. After this week, I wouldn't be the least bit surprised to find out that you really are a dragon and could shift anytime you wanted." Grandmother laughed, it was a sad sort of one, but he smiled when she looked at him. "We can go out of doors, I think, for this. I'm curious, that's all."

As they were headed out of the castle, Mom grabbed Amy's arm and hustled the two of them ahead of the rest of them. When she leaned in and spoke into her ear, he heard Amy laugh. Not just a giggle, though he did want to hear her do that sometime, but a full belly laugh that brought a smile to his face.

Once they were outside, Dad asked him to create a flame. Before he could do as asked, Amy asked him if the heat would harm the grounds. He didn't know, so he asked his mom. She told them that it would burn the earth.

"Then I'll make it. I've discovered, quite by accident, that I don't burn the earth when I make a flame. Also, Donka showed me different ways that I can float from different flames to get to where I'm going." Grandmother looked so excited that he wanted to have them hurry things along so that he could feel the excitement as well. "If you would step back, I don't want to accidentally hurt anyone that I care about."

The look she gave his grannie had him laughing out loud. He didn't even bother trying to hide his mirth as he would laugh just a little each time he thought about the expression on Amy's face and that of his great-grandmother. Leaving no doubt to anyone that she didn't care a bit about his grannie.

The fires, six of them, were set several feet apart. While standing behind her, he kissed her on the mouth quickly before moving back out of the way. He'd seen the flame that she used. Or at least one that she'd come to him in the form of his own fire.

"It's like riding — it must be like when you're your dragon, and you find a wind draft that you ride. I've seen birds do it, so that's where I got the idea of how to use it." Mom asked Amy if she could bounce, something that he thought it might be to her, to the last place without touching the middle pieces. "I'm afraid to, actually. I don't know how much time I have between jumps. It's finite. The amount of time I have between bounces. But the speed at which I can do it is amazing."

When she stepped into the open flame that she made, there were a few auditable gasps around the family when she was completely consumed by the flames and heat, her clothing nor her flesh seemingly unaffected by the heat and flames. He looked to the other end and saw her standing there, just outside the last flame still afire and smiling at them.

"Oh my goodness." When mom went to Amy, who had calmed the flames down to nothing more than a few places on her shorts, Amy handed her a small package. "What's this?"

"I noticed that you were out of tea, and I went to pick this brand up for you. I know how much you enjoyed it the other day when you shared with me and decided that I'd take a little side trip to get some." Mom looked at him and then at the small tin of tea that he knew for a fact was only sold in New

York at a specialty shop off the main drag. Mom kept staring at the tin. "It's the right brand, isn't it?"

"Yes. I mean…yes. Thank you…you were only gone for seconds. How did that happen?" Mom hugged her. "You know what? I don't really care. This is the greatest gift because you simply got it for me."

After another hug, they separated. Grannie looked as if she was going to say something, but one look from him had her close her mouth. It was then that he was worried that his grannie might try and harm Amy. Simply because she was a part of her daughter's family now. Dad asked her what would happen if there wasn't a flame for her to use.

"There is always something that has even a spark of fire. A car starting. A flare from an oven. Anything and everything I can take energy from to — that's what it is to me. A spark of energy. I never thought of that until just this second. It's not the heat that I thought that I needed, though I guess it's some of that, too, but the energy. It fuels me until the next jump." Dad asked her if she knew when she needed more. "Yes, the flames — again — get cooler, and I know that…I have discovered that if I don't make it, I won't die. The first time it happened to me, all I did was end up in a field somewhere until I could find another source. Thank you, Alex, that was extremely helpful."

As Amy explained what she had done to kill Grail, his dad came to talk to him. He had the strangest look on his face. Going a few hundred feet away from all the others, his dad asked him what his plans were for him and Amy.

"I don't know yet. We've agreed…she agreed to let me start over with her. I'm going to grovel for the rest of my days to make it so that I don't piss her off any more than I have already. Why do you ask?" He told him. "You think she'll be stronger when we mate? Dad, I don't know if you're aware of it now or not, but I think she's stronger than any of us, even together. She can use fire. I can as well, but she can manipulate it in ways that she can burn a body to nothing and not have to be a great hulking dragon while she's doing it. To the point that not even bone fragments would be found. I can burn a body, but there will be skeletal remains from it. Also, she's a bit more precise in her aim than I'll ever be."

"Does she scare you?" He didn't hesitate to tell his dad that he was terrified of her but was falling in love with her, too. "That's always good. You should start with that when you talk to her. Also, you might not be aware of this right now, but I think that any one of your brothers would murder you or at least attempt to murder you if you hurt her again. I would be first in line."

"And I shall allow them to do it too." Dad stared at him and then nodded. "All right. You didn't just bring me here to talk to me about how much I want to make Amy happy. What's going on?"

"She killed Grail. Do you have any idea what that means for the two of you? As a couple?" He shook his head. "His wealth, houses, money, as well as anything else he had acquired during his lifetime, is now yours. So is his magic. She will get it all, and I'm thinking that because of who she is, she'll share with you."

"And?" Dad looked to where Grannie was standing before speaking again. Staggering back, just a little from the news, he stood there reeling from it as what he'd been told settled in his mind. "Dad, I don't know what to say about that. How did you find out that Grannie was funding Grail to kill us off? I mean, you said that because of their relationship, Grannie would be drained as well. How did you figure it out?"

"When I shot him all those years ago, Grail, I mean, he recuperated at your great-grandmother's home. I have only recently been made aware of that. I don't know that your grandmother knows about that either." He asked him if Mom knew. "She doesn't want to believe it either, but she knows. It's going to be something to think about. When your grandmother puts her name in the book about Amy killing Grail, watch Tisha. See if what I think will happen does. She'll be drained. I would imagine by a great deal. But I don't know."

"I'll keep an eye on her. Dad, don't be near her. Warn the others, too. To stay as far away from Grannie as possible when her name is added to the book." Grandmother called them all to come to her when she picked up her pin. Nodding once at his dad when everyone moved away from his great-grandmother, he focused his attention on Amy.

"All right. I just need a name, Amy. Your full name for the record." Amy told her, and Fowler realized that it was the first time he'd heard her full name. Fowler knew, too, that he'd never heard her last name until that moment. "Amelia Jane Stocker Walsh, destroyed—"

Grandmother got no further than that. When

she moved forward, drawing something from behind her over her head, Fowler did something that he hoped he wouldn't regret for the rest of his days.

With just enough room, he ran, and using the table there as a jumping point, he shifted into his dragon and swooped down toward his great-grandmother all at one time. Tasting blood and evilness, he knew that he'd just snapped her head off with his great teeth. The very idea that he'd had to keep her from harming Amy was to block her. But he did more than that. Fowler beheaded his great-grandmother, and his dragon crunched up her head in his mouth before swallowing it.

Chapter 4

Amy sat very still while conversations, mostly about her and Fowler, went on around her. There was talk about the great-grandmother, but they'd not asked her yet what she'd figured out, so she didn't give them the information that would no doubt in her mind change a great many things about what had transpired to get them to the point they were now. And she'd bet well beyond here, too.

"Are you needing anything?" Each of the Walsh men, the boys they were called, had stopped by her seating place to ask her if she needed anything. She had plates of food on the bench beside her, apples and oranges beside her, as well as several bottles of water. The only person who hadn't been by, and she was beginning to worry, was Fowler. He was still in a meeting with a bunch of arrogant asses that had shown up right after the death of Tisha.

"I'm fine. Just wondering what is going on with Fowler." Dyson, this time, told her that he didn't know, but it couldn't last much longer. "It's been three hours. I'm going to go in there and remove their heads if they don't get out here and explain shit to us."

He laughed and stayed with her when his mom came to sit with her. Sending Dyson on a small errand, she asked Storm what she was going to tell her. And not to fuck around with it. To just tell her.

"I remember that about you. All right. He's being charged with murdering—excuse me. I'm still speaking here." Amy told her to come with her. She wanted to have witnesses when heads were rolling. "Oh, goody. This will be fun. Do I need to be a dragon, or have you got this?"

"I have it." Shoving her hands against the large doors that had kept them all out of whatever they were doing, she felt a slight resistance, but not enough to slow her down. Once she had everyone's attention on the other side of the door, she smiled. "What the royal fuck is going on in here that you think that you're going to charge my mate with something."

"Not that it's any of your business, young lady, but he did kill a standing member of the queen's family." She pointed out to the man, talking that Fowler, too, was a part of the royal family. "We're well aware of his connections. What I don't understand is why you think you should be privy to anything that goes on behind closed doors. Which you're going to close again on your way out of here."

"I'm not leaving. And my connection is that I, too, am part of the family. Fowler is my mate." She glanced at him, but she could tell that he was nervous. "Did you, by chance, ask his dragon what that old bitch tasted like when he killed the woman trying to kill us? Or what I might have gotten from Grail when I removed his head the other day? Nope, you're only focusing on things that are the end product, in this case, their deaths, instead of why we were brought to the point of needing their asses taken out." Storm touched her shoulder before speaking to her.

"This is supposed to be very formal, honey. I'm not saying that I agree with that, but you might want to—never mind. You go and get my son free, please." Amy kissed Storm on the cheek before turning back to the men.

"Did you know that Grail, a rouge dragon that you've been trying to have arrested or whatever it is that you do with criminals, had insider information when he was killed? Again, by me? He was to kill Fowler and remove his head. Then, while the family was grieving, because who wouldn't at such a death, he was going to help take over the kingdom and become the ruler for all times. That's the really shortened version of their plans. Tisha was helping him know things like where they were. What they were up to and what would kill them. I think that makes her a bad guy, but then, I'm just marrying into this family and not really been around all that much yet. I think this has gone on long enough that we should just skip to the juicy part. And do you want to know who would be right there at Grail's side when this ended their way? You don't know so I'll explain it to you more. Tisha was the ringleader in all this shit going down. The reason that she showed up when she did, conveniently as it was planned by Grail and her to be there for Fowler's funeral. Imagine her surprise when she found out that not only was her oldest great-grandson still alive but, and here is the part that made her think she could do this on her own. Grail had failed her by getting himself killed while he was at it. Sort of like that old joke. He had one job and fucked that up too." She laughed, but the men didn't.

"You just expect us to believe you on this?" Amy told the man that she was getting really sick of people calling her a liar. "I don't really care what you are sick of. This man killed a dragon of great value to us."

"Then we can only assume that you're a part of the problem." He asked her what she meant. "If you're not a part of the solution then you're part of the problem. My grannie said that a lot when I was growing up. I wanted to always be a part of the solution. She had a bit of a temper on her so I was forever trying to be on her good side. And that's what Fowler and I are, on the good side of this shit. You, questioning him like you are makes me think that you have lost your ever loving mind, especially if you think that you're going to get away with putting Fowler in prison for killing off the old bitch and her plans. Do you really think that we're going to just allow you to go ahead with whatever stupid plans the woman had worked out? I don't think so. Here is what I suggest you do. Get your heads together and be happy that you're not chomped up by a dragon too."

"What of that plan?" The man standing closest to the first talker smiled at her. "My name is Girthy.

I'm part of the dragon council. This man here is Tobler, and the man to my right is Saul. What do you mean by saying that she'd be killing off dragons? I've not heard of that before." Fowler cleared his throat.

"Because you won't allow me to speak. I'm amazed that anything gets done between the three of you the way you bicker and bitch at every little thing that is said between you. I tried to tell you when I was brought in here. Then again, when you took a small break. A break, I might add, that I was denied. Now my mate comes in, and suddenly, you don't know what's going on around the kingdom. Fat lot of good it does dragons if you're there to suppose to listen to their grievances without them being allowed to speak." She could have kissed Fowler when he smiled at her. "Go ahead, honey. Tell them what you and I found out when we were killing the bad guys that these people don't seem to know a thing about."

She had to clear her throat twice before she could speak. The way that Fowler was looking at her gave her the shakes. Why? She didn't have a clue, but she kind of liked the feeling. Amy turned to the men.

"Tisha was retired when it was realized that she was abusing her powers as queen. Not many people knew that, but she didn't care all that much for her forced retirement and her decrease in magic that came with it." They all turned to Morning when she entered the room, confirming what she had said. But it wasn't public knowledge because she hadn't wanted her mother embarrassed.

"It wasn't so much the forced retirement as it turned out, but the fact that she could no longer take as much magic as she wanted from underlings she called them when they came to her with issues. So she approached Grail."

Amy knew that this part was going to be hurtful to both Morning and Storm, but she needed to let them know how long the plotting and planning for the takeover had been going on.

"Grail, sadly, was stupid. And I don't mean that in a derogatory way. He was stupid. He could neither read nor write and depended on Tisha to tell him just what was going on all the time. And in doing so, she made the plight of her dismissal from her job worse than it really was. He, of course, believed her. Also, the other things that she told him. How that they together would have dragons that would answer only to them. Also, and this one boggles my mind completely that they'd kill off all the other dragons in the world, including her daughter, the previous queen, as well as Storm. I don't even want to think about how much darker this world would be without the magic of the dragons." Girthy asked why she thought that the magic would be gone. "Do you even know how magic works? Or do you care? Christ, man. Magic is everywhere. And with the death of all dragons, it would deplete the magic to the point— You've surely heard about the bees and how the earth is losing them. Also what the effect of them being gone will do to the earth, right?"

"Yes, something along the lines of there would be no produce because there are no bees to pollinate things." She told him that it wasn't something like that, but that was it. "Yeah, I heard. We'll all starve. I don't know if you realize this or not, but we have this entire realm here to live in."

"You think so? Well, I've got news for you, buddy. If no one has magic or believes in it, you don't exist, either. The only reason that this realm is here and working is because of the magic that is in my world, too. People believe in it and thus makes it real. However, if they are starving and have nothing to believe in, the poof, it's all gone." He looked at Morning again, and so did Amy. "Tell the idiot here thinking that the realm was specially built for him in his pea-sized brain that I'm right."

"Not only is she right, but I've never heard it explained quite that way before. No magic, no belief then there is no reason for us to be around." Morning sat down in one of the few chairs in the room. Storm sat next to her with Alex at her side. "Tell him the part where if my mother had succeeded, where he'd be. She'd start killing off dragons here so that she'd have free reign of this place. She'd need a place to hide out, and since this place has the most magic for now, she would suck it all dry faster. That would include those three. And don't forget to explain too how my mother killed my mate and tried, daily, from what I've gathered, to kill off Alex as well. He's a crafty vampire and knew to watch out for her ways."

Amy thought that Morning and Storm were taking this way better than she would have after finding out that someone had murdered their mates. When Storm stood up, a great pause settled over the room, and Amy was nervous. If one of them decided that she was full of shit, she'd be toast. Burnt toast.

"My daughter-in-law has done more for our kind in the few months she's been hanging out with my family than you have in all the centuries you've been at the council. Kind of makes me wonder why we even have you around." Storm walked to the three men and hugged Fowler. Then she turned to them again. "Get your head out of your asses before I have to do that for you. They're dead. What we should be focusing on is not that they're dead, thankfully, but what sort of damage had they done before anyone noticed."

"I have a list." Alex handed the list that he had to Fowler. "And I'd like to recommend that we have Amy and Fowler look into these things. At a date that will be determined later."

When Fowler burst out laughing, she looked at him. At his wink at her, it still took her mind a few seconds to catch up to what they were talking about. Sex. They all thought that they were going to have sex. And that it might take…she was just about to say something to the effect of she would decide now when the date was when Girthy picked up a sword that she'd not noticed before.

"That is the weaponry that was being wielded by Trisha when she meant to kill me. How did she get it here is what we should be asking, too. Isn't this room supposed to be weapon-free or something along those lines?" Amy looked closer at the sword and noticed that it was missing a gem. "I've seen this piece before. But only in that dragon book that you guys gave Fowler. It belonged to the Starter, I believe.

Moving closer to the sword, she felt the presence of Fowler close behind her and pulled the long-forgotten orb from her pocket. She had meant so many times over the last few days to toss it out, thinking that it was nothing. Putting the gem in the space where she thought that it had come from, she wasn't prepared for the thing to rise up in the room and spin at a dizzying speed that knocked her on her ass. The last thing that she remembered was Fowler saying 'Oh fuck' and Morning laughing.

~*~

The place Fowler was looking at was just what he wanted. The next step, he supposed, was waiting for Amy to wake up so that she could tell him if he had terrible taste or not. Grinning, he didn't doubt that she'd tell him exactly what she thought of the place when she saw it. He heard her stirring and turned around at the table he'd been using for a desk to see if she needed anything.

"I feel all right. Confused, I guess. Do you know why I was tossed around like a feather in a fan factory? When was that anyway? Hopefully, not

too long ago that I've been sleeping for days." He
thought about what she'd described and laughed.
He told her that he'd brought her here about three
hours ago. "Good, I guess. And that was not funny.
My head feels like it's been used as a bowling ball,
and I feel like my skin is trying to get off my body for
a better one."

"Okay, I want to address the fact that your
body is perfect, from what I've seen of it, and no one
will be able to find a better one." Fowler frowned.
"I forgot where I was going with our conversation.
It doesn't matter. I have something for your head,
but I don't know if you're going to like it any better
than I did when I complained about having a sore
head. I didn't get tossed around as much as you did,
but—I have something for your head." He handed
her the wet cloth that he'd been handed earlier. "I
was told that the magic has to settle before you can
have medications. Not that they've ever worked on
me before, but that was what I was—"

"Fowler." His mouth snapped close. "What are
you nervous about? You're babbling like a kid. What
else is going on that you're afraid to tell me?"

"I'm not sure that I'm afraid of telling you
anything so much as I don't know you well enough

to know how you're going to react. But I did find us a house." He handed her his laptop and laid on the bed beside her. He was careful of not getting too close, yet close enough that he could 'accidentally' brush up against her if the occasion presented itself. "It has a lot of space for us to grow in. I mean, the yard does. The house is all right, but the kitchen will need some work. Actually, the entire house will need some work. Do you cook?" She said if she had to. "I'm the same way. If I don't have to cook, then I'm not going to do it. There are seven bedrooms, not so thrilled about their size, but I guess...it's the yard that I suppose I really liked about the house."

"Why are you looking for us a house? And by us, I'm not sure there is an us yet to get ahead of yourself." He didn't point out that everyone had heard her telling the faerie that she was going to be their future queen, but he showed her the other houses that he was looking into. "If all you're into is the yard on each of these places, perhaps it would be better if you just bought a plot of land and built on it. You can make the house as big as you want then."

"Excellent. I have just the land—see how brilliant you are? What has taken me four hours to come to, you had it in less than ten minutes." She glared at him. "I'm stalling. I don't know how you're going to feel about the information that I have about the tossing thing."

"Is it bad?" He said it would depend on her. "All right. I can understand that. The sword, it has something to do with it, doesn't it?"

"All of it, as a matter of fact. Also, I have been reading over the book that Grandmother gave you, and more information has been added since the tossing thing. About the Starter, you called her." She asked him what happened. "According to the new part written, she disappeared in the sword that she used to give fire to families once she was able to give the fire to them. The sword was found in her hut when she disappeared, and no one knew anything that had happened to her. I'm not sure about a lot of the things written there, but I'm to understand that you are to take over the job that she developed, I guess you could call it, for you. The job description isn't just you going around lighting dragons like you mentioned to my family. It's more than that now. You'll have to go over it. I only got the newest version of the book, so you'll know more about what's been added or not. But it does sound like she's been awaiting you to be born and to find me."

"When you say more, what do you mean?" Fowler told her that he wasn't sure, but there was a mention of the rules being updated by her. There was also a lot more magic to be given to the new Starter. She asked him for the book, and he handed it to her with the page open. "There is a great deal of information here that wasn't before. Like you said, it tells where she'd gone when she disappeared. Do you have any idea why she picked me to do this?"

"There is a lot of stuff there that I don't even understand right now. And to be honest with you, I'm not sure how you would understand some of the rules when you're not only not a dragon, and you can't fly either. Or at least I don't think so." He looked at her for a few moments. "Can you?"

"I wouldn't even begin to know how to get started on seeing if I could fly." She laid back on the bed and closed her eyes. "I'm suddenly exhausted again. Like I could sleep for days and not feel like it was nearly enough."

He watched her falling asleep. Fowler had never done that before, watching someone sleep. Not that he would admit it to anyone, especially not Amy, but he had wished people—women—were asleep so that he could sneak out of their bed and house. Smiling as he got off the bed and went to the computer again, he decided to look up land rather than houses. She'd been right in that. He did want more than just a little patch of land.

As dragons, they couldn't fly where they'd be seen around in the earth's realm. Maybe on a cloudy day, but you'd be taking a huge chance at still being seen. However, in the other realm, they could all fly together should they wish, and no one would care. In fact, he thought that some of the people came out to watch them as if it were a holiday. Fowler did so love being his other self. And having a large yard meant that he could shift and stretch out on his grass where no one would see him. Provided it put up a tall fence around his yard. Fowler glanced over at Amy when she stirred again. Something occurred to him then.

It wasn't his yard. Not his house. He didn't have a car that was his. He had someone to share it with. Not just his things but his life, too. He also figured out that he was looking forward to sharing his things. Their things. Even things that he'd had well before meeting and falling in love—something else he discovered too: he was in love with Amy and was overjoyed by that feeling. Thinking about his parents in that moment, he remembered times when they shared things too.

They were forever snuggling on the couch together. They went on dates to this day. Going to see a movie or just out to dinner was something that they did at least once a week. He'd bring Mom flowers for no reason at all. And on days like her birthday, he'd go all out in giving her gifts, flowers, and other things throughout the entire month. Mom was the same. She had even been known to bring Dad flowers, too. And gifts of candy when she'd find some special candies for him.

Dad loved chocolate. The only thing that Fowler thought he loved more was Mom. But she hated all things chocolate. It didn't matter if it only had a bit of the dark, rich stuff on it. She wouldn't even taste it. However, he knew for a fact that when his mom went to the café in town, she would pick up more than half the sweet treats that she'd bring home for her and Dad, there would be more chocolate than anything. Then, she acted confused when he told her what she'd purchased.

Fowler had always thought that his mother was dumb, the way she'd do that week after week. But now he saw it as a way for the two of them to have fun. His dad, too, when it came to buying something mom dearly loved. They had been romantic his entire life, and he'd missed every bit of it.

Shaking his head, he went back to looking for land for him and Amy. Fowler was looking forward to creating memories with Amy as much as he was just about anything that he'd ever done before. It got him to thinking about why he'd been so set against having a mate in the first place. Fowler figured that he was just a selfish bastard and had changed his ways. Yes, he thought and was looking forward to changing more each day for his Amy.

His mind did wander more than it should have while sitting there. Four times, the computer had gone to sleep on him, and he would berate himself for not focusing on the task at hand. Then, twenty minutes later, he'd have to wake up the computer again and try and remember why he was on the page that it woke up to.

"If we have sex, will I get more power or magic—whatever you're calling it?" He nearly fell backward on his chair when Amy spoke from behind him. He had just touched the button on his mouse to turn down the volume. "Well? It's a legitimate question. Yes or no?" He had to drag his mind out of the slutty filled thought that he'd had to answer her.

"Yes. I don't know how much or what it would be. The very fact that you have vampire magic is something I don't think anyone could have counted on." This time, he decided he'd stay on the chair and turned it around to face her rather than getting into bed with her. "We can go into the yard and try out things that I can do. Though that wouldn't count if we haven't made love yet. It has its appeal, to have sex outside, but there are just too many people working in—I babble when I'm nervous, I guess."

"You seem to be nervous all the time. Or is it just me?" Before he could think up another reason that he was nervous, he answered her truthfully that he was indeed nervous all the time around her. "Why?"

"Why...well, that's a good question. It has about a million and a half answers in my head right now. You make me nervous—totally not your fault— but I'm worried that I'll be a prick again. I'm getting better at not lashing out at everyone, thanks to you. I'm nervous because I want, now anyway, to be a good mate to you. Supportive. A sounding board. Believe it or not, I only just realized how romantic my parents are for each other. I didn't want to notice it more than I just realized it, I think." She asked him why. "I was angry. I don't know when that started to be the way that I greeted each day. Nor how it got to be so out of control for me. No, not angry. It was more than that. I was just hateful to everyone and anything. I have been known to knock doors off of their frames because they might not have opened easily. When I think back on how pissed off I was all the time, I can't believe that someone didn't bash my head in sooner. Or, for that matter, removed my head." He put his hands over his throat and had to count to ten when he couldn't breathe. I don't want to think about that if I don't have to."

"You were over the top with being pissed off. I talked to your brothers a lot while I was recuperating. They said it seemed like since forever that you had a kind word to anyone. Even strangers, I guess. They could depend on you to be there for them, but you'd make them feel like shit for asking for help. That is not a way to treat a family, I hope you've come to realize." He said that he had, and while he didn't like knowing that his brothers felt that way, he was happy for her telling him. "The person that I think you hurt the most, however, was your grandmother. I'm just putting that out there, but if and that's a big if we come together, I'm going to insist that you visit her at least weekly. She told me that you never come to see her unless she commands you to. That's just fucking sad. My grandparents are all gone, and I'd give just about anything to have them back with me. Even if it's for a day. I'd tell them how much I loved them and loved being around them. You might have more of a chance to tell her that, but someday, and you never know, she'll be gone then what will you do? Hurt, that's how you'll feel."

He didn't say anything but stared at Amy when she told him about his grandmother. In his head, he remembered several times, dozens of times, when she'd ask him to come visit her, and he blew her off. Sometimes, he remembered telling her that he'd go see her and simply not show—it had been his plan all along to not go. It hurt his own heart that he'd been so cruel because that's what it had been, cruelty not to go and see her more often than he did. Amy said his name, and he looked at her before speaking.

"You're right. I've been...I wish I had an excuse for being that way. I don't have one. I don't even remember why I acted that way around her. She always made me feel welcome to go and see her. There was never a time when she had hurt my feelings when I didn't go see her either. I just wouldn't go because I didn't want to. Like I thought I had better things to do than to sit around with her. That isn't an excuse that I can live with now. I will see her as much as I can from now on. And whenever she asks." She asked him if he'd seen his grandfather. "He was gone before I was born. I just remembered that I'm named for him. But…grandmother would tell me stories about him when I was a child. I remember those. And remember being such a shit to her when I was bored out of my mind about…would you mind if I went to see her now? I feel the need to get a hug from her."

"If you don't go now, I'm going to brain you. Of course, go see her." He stood up and sat down. "Now, Fowler. Go see your grandmother."

"Come with me." She started to shake her head. "Please. I owe…I'm not sure what I can call it, but I feel like I've had some kind of breakthrough with you by my side. I know you're not willing to be by my side as yet, but you hopefully will be." He grinned. "Come with me. Please. I want you to be there when I tell her what I've been thinking."

"If you embarrass me in any way, I'm going to really brain you. While I have an idea that you have a brain, I'm not so sure how much you use it." He agreed with her as he pulled her up from the bed. "What is wrong with you?"

He didn't know. But he was in love, and he wanted the world to know it. Picking her up in his arms, he swung her around. Slightly afraid of dropping her, he stopped moving and kissed her on the mouth. However, just as he was pulling away, Amy wrapped her arms around his shoulders and looked at him. Fowler let her. Let her see any flaws she could find, too.

"Let's go see your grandmother." He nodded but didn't move. "We'll go see her and then come back here. I want to have sex with you. Don't call it making love, Fowler. I don't know that I'm ready for that. But I would like to have sex with you. To fill a part of me that I hadn't realized felt empty until now."

"Why see my grandmother first, then? Not that I mind, but why?" She shrugged and told him she didn't know, but it seemed important. "All right. It's nagging at me, too, that I see her."

When he put her down on the floor, she took his hand into hers. When he kissed the back of hers, she did the same to his. The part of his heart that belonged to her, nearly all of it, jumped a little, and he felt like a new man. Fowler could get used to these new and amazing feelings, and he was going to find a new one with her daily.

Going to the other realm wasn't difficult. He found that it was easier to go there than to come back some years ago. But today, it was entirely different. Getting to the realm felt like not only was it marred with things in the way, things blocking the path, but the magic coming from the other realm felt like it was depleted in some way.

As soon as they were in her drawing room, Amy pulled away from him to find the kitchen help. He didn't know why, but it seemed important to him that he stayed in the room he'd entered. Walking around it, looking for anything out of place, he was shocked to see not only her favorite chair knocked over, but the stuffing had been pulled from it. That was when Amy yelled for him to go to the kitchen.

Grandmother was on the floor with her hand bleeding. Picking her up as Amy told him to do, Fowler sat her on the counter and laid her head on his shoulder. She'd been bleeding for a while, he thought, if the way she was weak was any indication. That was when he noticed that it wasn't her hand that she'd cut but her wrist. Amy asked him if he could heat up a knife for her.

"You do it. Your aim will be better." He didn't have any idea why Amy needed the knife hot. He was too worried about his grandmother right now to think beyond the blood still flowing from her wrist. "I can lick this closed, but I'm worried about something...what did she do?"

"It looks like she was making herself something to eat." The knife was heated to white hot by Amy wrapping her hand around the blade to heat it and she told him to hold onto his grandmother. "This is going to hurt her."

Amy laid the blade over the gaping wound, and he had to hold tightly onto his grandmother when she screamed, trying her best to get away from the pain. When she fainted, he picked her up and took her to the living room to lay her on the couch. While not leaving her side, Fowler reached out to his mom and told her what was going on. She appeared in the room with his dad in seconds.

Letting his mom take over, he stood out of the way, ready to do whatever was needed of him. Dad offered his blood, but it was decided that since they didn't know how it would affect her, they decided that for now, they'd just use a bit of hers. Mom was even hesitant to do that.

"I'll do it." Without waiting for anyone to reply, Amy put her hand over his grandmother's heart and told her to wake up. "Come on now. You're scaring the shit out of everyone."

Grandmother opened her eyes and looked at Amy. After calling her rude, she asked if she was all right. Fowler fell to the floor on his butt. He was so happy to hear his grandmother awake that his knees simply gave out on him. When asked if he was all right, he nodded. His ability to form words was lost to him as he was so relieved to know that she was going to be all right now. Mom asked her what she'd been doing.

"I was going to make me something to eat, and one of the faeries brought in an avocado for me to try. I watched a couple of videos—I feel really stupid now—on how to take out the seed. I should have known better. I'm a grown assed woman, and I did something incredibly stupid. My goodness, it happened so quickly that I didn't have time to even call out to anyone. I used a knife on the seed to pull it free and missed." Amy told her that she was glad that she was all right but not to do that again. "I promise you I won't. I would someday like to try one, but I think that I'll leave that to the cooks here."

"You're going to need to rest, Mom. For a while until you're able to regain your strength. Why don't you come home with me and —" Grandmother shook her head and told her that she would heal faster here. "Then someone is going to need to be with you. I don't know what is going to happen with you losing so much blood, but I'd feel better if —"

"We'll stay." Fowler looked at Amy when she spoke. "There are some things that Fowler and I have to do, but we can easily do that from anywhere. I think that staying here and helping her heal will be good for all of us. It'll be like downtime for the three of us, and we can get to know her better. Besides, Fowler was just telling me that he wanted to spend more time with his grandmother, and this will work out better than before."

"You want to spend time with me, Fowler?" The excitement in Grandmother's voice hurt him. He really had been a shithead to his grandmother, and telling her that he really did, she asked him to give her a hug. "I need this more than anything, I believe. Yes, this will be perfect. I'll get to know Amy better and spend some much-needed time with my grandson, too. Oh yes, this is perfect."

There was no reason for them to go home to pack. Everything they would need for an extended stay with his grandmother would be provided by the faeries that were here. After getting his grandmother settled in her bed, they talked for most of the evening. Mom and Dad left just after midnight, and he couldn't have been happier than he was at that moment that not only had he gotten his head out of his ass but that Amy was going to make him a better man. Something that he thought he'd never aspired to before in his life.

Settling into one of the many bedrooms in the castle, he reached for Amy when she lay down beside him. She was warm, as he was, so they lay there without the benefit of blankets until the sun came up. He knew that she'd long since fallen asleep, but he didn't want to get up just yet. He thought of all the things that had changed in the few short hours of him realizing how much he loved Amy. Being in love with someone was much better than he'd ever imagined it to be.

Fowler thought of all the things that would be theirs once they were together. Not just the magic, though, that was something that he was thinking about. It was children. He'd not once in all his adult life thought about being a father. He didn't think about what his children would have been either. Dragons, of course. His mom had told him that since dragons were stronger than humans in the bloodline, their kids had turned out to be what she was. He'd bet that they'd be the same, too, when he fathered them.

Then he thought about it and wondered if that would change since Amy was magical too. He didn't yet know what kind of things she'd be able to do as the Starter, but he'd be willing to lay his life on the line so that she could and would be able to save him. Thinking about her shifting into a dragon thrilled him to think about, too. His dad couldn't, of course, but he was just as powerful as their mom. It gave him something wonderful to think about.

As he was getting out of the bed to go and check on a couple of things that he'd only then remembered, he found the books that he'd read as a younger man. Fowler didn't have any idea why he thought of the herb book and the spell book that had been a long-ago relative, but he sat in one of the chairs that had been his grandfathers he'd been told and opened the book about herbs up. Smiling to himself while he read the forward in the book, he wondered what his dad would say if he knew that he was reading a book that had been around longer than he'd been. And his dad was an ancient.

The sun was setting when he heard Amy coming down the hall. Putting the book away, he told her what he'd been doing. After checking on his grandmother and finding her in the yard with the faeries, the three of them decided to hike to the mountaintop to do some exploring. Something that apparently his grandmother had wanted to do with him for decades, and he'd been too much of a shit to go with her. He also was able to gather up some mushrooms to take back to the castle for the faeries to cook for their lunch. He loved being with these two women.

Chapter 5

Realizing that she needed to shower in the worst kind of way—her body felt dirty and dusty, she went to the bedroom where they had planned to stay with his grandmother and turned on the water. The pressure, she was sure, was hard enough that she could massage each and every one of her muscles without ever touching them with her fingers.

The water felt glorious. Amy didn't know if there was such a thing as magical water, but she'd believe it right now if someone told her there was. Standing under the hot spray for a few minutes before she felt someone touch her. She turned to stare at Fowler.

"I know that I'm sort of crowding you, but I need to touch you. I need to get cleaned up, too. Like you told grandmother, you feel like you're covered in dust. My other half feels like he's been, I'm not sure. He feels like he needs to mark you in some way, too. All right?" Looking him up and down, she turned away from him. Christ, the man was just too delicious for words. His small chuckle made her turn back to him.

"I'm not having sex with you in the shower. First of all, I don't care what you're thinking about marking me, and secondly…well, secondly, no shower sex. So if that was what you had in mind when you suggested this, then get the fuck out now."

He reached above her head. Her heart was pounding, and she was pretty sure he knew it. But other than showing her the bottle of shampoo, he didn't touch her. She was both glad and disappointed at the same time.

"I told you I just want to shower and wash my hair and get cleaned up. I'm sorry I don't have anything but my shampoo, but I've never stayed here with a woman before. I don't know that anyone has but my mom and dad. I'm babbling again." She found that hard to believe that he'd not had sex. "I'm not saying I didn't have sex, love. I just never brought anyone to this place. At my home, either. I think my mom would have killed me. Plus, it just didn't feel right. Let me help you with your hair first."

His fingers started at her scalp and moved over her head in deep but gentle strokes. He massaged behind her ears, over her crown, and finally along her neck. Holding on, the only way she knew that she was able to stand upright, Amy let him do what he wanted to her.

When he told her to rinse, she was putty and had to brace herself by holding onto the tiled wall while doing what he asked. Then, when he washed it the second time, giving her head the same wonderful all-over touch, she had to lean her head against the tile in addition to holding on. Rinsing her hair out, she felt as if she'd been dipped in a total body wrap of warmth and sexual need.

He handed her a natural sponge and a nice loofah, and then he squirted soap on it. He apologized again for not having anything but his scent, but he'd take care of that for her soon. He kissed the back of her neck. After nodding to him, she worked the soap all over her body where she could. When he lifted her arm above her head, she had to ask him twice what he'd said.

"I'm going to massage your arms from one end to the other. Once, when I was having muscle aches, I was able to have a nurse — that's all she was, a nurse massage my arms from fingers to shoulder." She turned her head to look at him. "You can't manage this on your own. I promise you, Amy, I'm only trying to help you relax a bit. I know how tense I am."

"All right." She let him massage her arms and knew that, on some level, this was kind of weird, but she had never felt so…so very relaxed in her life. He held her to his body to work the muscles under her left arm, and she felt his cock brush against her.

She stiffened slightly, and he murmured that he was sorry and pulled away. By the time he was finished, he had brushed against her three more times. She was beginning to think that this was going to get her into major trouble. And when he dropped to his knees in front of her, she backed against the wall. Amy watched as he rubbed the sponge up her leg and then his other hand.

"I've been thinking about my grannie. That she'd been at this trying to kill us all off for a while. I can't help but think that when she drew her sword that she meant to kill you first, finding you to be a bigger threat than my mom and grandmother were." All she could do was nod at him as she sat down on the little bench in the stall. Amy wasn't sure but she thought that the stall had gotten bigger, at least wider than it had been before. "Do you know what her plans might have been after I was dead? I'm making conversation right now because all I have in my mind about you is lust and taking you right here on the seat."

"Fowler." She heard her voice and wondered for a second who had spoken so breathlessly. It couldn't have been her, her mind told her. She wasn't interested in having shower sex. But then it was all she could think about. Her entire body felt as if it were on fire. She had to close her eyes or risk begging him to take her. It didn't help.

Every time his hands moved over her leg, she felt her muscles tighten. Then his hand would follow the path of the other hand, and she would melt again. He moved up and down her leg over and over until she thought she'd scream, beg him to take her. When he moved up her thighs, he asked her to open her legs, and she was glad they were in the shower. She was sure that had they been anywhere else, he'd see how wet she was. Amy felt like it was pouring out of her. She was so needy.

As his hand moved over her smooth shins, his cheek brushed her thigh. Every time he moved along the inner part of her leg, she would anticipate him touching her pussy. But he didn't. When he told her to turn so he could finish the job, she nearly sobbed in relief. But the tension only got more intense.

His chin touched the back of her knees, and she wobbled. When he lifted one foot up then the other, rubbed his thumb over the bottom of her feet, and massaged her toes, she had to bite her lip. By the time he started to run his hands over her calves, Amy knew that she was nearly to the point of throwing him to the floor and taking him.

"I broke my arm." Her mind was a haze of lust, her body on meltdown, and she had to ask him what he said. "I broke my arm when I was about seven. I had to take baths, which I now find that I'd love to take with you until it healed. I could have shifted and healed, but there wasn't the room, and I would have been caught. To this day, I think about that every time I see that tree in my parents' yard."

His mouth grazed along her ass. His teeth nipped at her flesh. She couldn't move. Couldn't breathe. No, it wasn't that she couldn't, but that she simply didn't remember how. His hands moved up her thigh, and she moaned his name. Turning around, she looked down at him as he stared up at her.

His hand was wrapped around his cock as he sat on her knees. He moved up and down his shaft slowly as she watched him. The warm water and soap making his sliding like that much easier. When he stopped, she looked at his face.

"I can smell you. You are as aroused as I am, aren't you?" She nodded, not capable of speech still. "I know you said no shower sex, but I would love to taste you. Sip from you until I come."

Her legs trembled as his head moved forward. Opening her legs for him, she curled her hand into his hair to hold on. When he suckled her clit into his mouth, she came screaming his name. But he didn't stop.

His mouth ate at her. Devoured her until she was coming again. Every time she came, every time she exploded into his mouth, he continued to eat her, drink from her. When his finger slipped into her, she started to beg him. She had no idea what he thought of her, but she wanted him inside of her, over her, and even behind her. He pulled away suddenly, and she whimpered.

But he stood and took her mouth just as voraciously. His cock rubbed against her belly, and she reached down and wrapped her hand around him. He was so thick that she could barely touch her finger to her thumb. He tore his mouth from hers.

"Christ," he said before cupping her ass and lifting her. "I need you. Please. Please, I need to be inside of you."

"Yes. Please. I need you, too." Lifting her higher above his cock, he brought her down hard onto him, impaled her over his cock, and she came again. When her back touched the tile, he pressed her hard against it, his cock throbbed within her.

"I can't be gentle. I can't…Christ, touching you like that, running my hands over your body like I did… Then you came in my mouth. I thought for sure that I was going to come all over the shower. I want to fuck you until you can't say another word to me." He moved into her, filling her over and over as he spoke. "I'm sorry, baby, but I can't wait."

He slammed into her. His cock filled her with every stroke. She threw back her head when he slid his mouth along her chin and to her throat. Giving her all to him she wrapped her hand onto his head.

"Please," she begged him. "I need you to… please, Fowler, make me yours." He licked the pulse she could feel pounding at her throat. His teeth scraped along her neck, and she tightened her grip on his head. When he sank his teeth into her and bit her hard enough that she was sure to draw blood, she screamed again, coming hard enough that she saw stars dance in her vision.

He lifted his head and looked at her. His cock was still hard and moving inside of her. Blood, her blood dripped from his lip. His eyes darker now seemed to reach into her soul.

"Bite me. I want you to bite me hard and draw blood. Please, baby, I want you to sink your teeth into my flesh and drink from me." She nodded and licked her lips. "Do it. Now, do it."

She licked his throat, not really sure she could do it, but when he commanded her again, the need to do as he asked, no demanded of her, she did it. Not sure what would happen, Amy did as she'd been commanded.

Her teeth punctured his flesh, and his blood filled her mouth. Sucking deeply, she moaned when his taste filled her. Drawing again, she felt his mouth do the same to her own throat, and she dug her hands into his shoulder and tightened around him.

When he came, she came with him. Her body felt each stroke of his cock, his cum as he filled her. When he licked her throat, he pulled her from his wound and looked into her eyes. She was right. He could see deep into her soul. And she knew on some level that there would never be another secret between the two of them ever again. Amy was glad, too.

"Mine. You're mine. Do you understand that?" She nodded. "Say it. Tell me you're mine."

"Yours. I'm yours." He took her mouth again. His body took her as well. Even as he came again, she knew that things were different. That there would never be anyone else and that this man was going to love her forever. As she came with him, his name sounding loudly from her lips, she knew that she didn't care at all. Closing her eyes, Amy let herself slip away, knowing that Fowler would keep her safe.

~*~

The area that the two of them were in seemed ideal. Fowler had shifted to his dragon when they first came out here because Amy wanted to have a look at him, and he'd stayed that way while she practiced the things that he'd suggested to her to try. So far, she was more powerful than he was in some things, but in others, she only had to touch him and bring more magic to herself.

They were sitting on the lawn with snacks for

her while she rested on the blanket that had been brought to her. The faeries were going out of their way to treat her with anything that she wanted. He loved the fact that they were excited to be the ones serving her. He smiled when she asked them to bring him something to eat, too.

"Oh." Donka looked at him and then back at Amy. She asked what was going on. "He is a dragon, my lady. He would...his appetite is much more than yours."

Amy looked at him confused, but she seemed to understand when he shifted to his other self and picked up the bowl of grapes that had been brought too. Nodding once, she asked the little ones if they had had to feed him before.

"Nay, my lady. We've not had to provide for dragons in a very long time. There aren't as many as there used to be, of course, but it would take a great many resources that we don't have here to fill one. They are good about being human-looking when they come here. However, I must confess, it is wonderful to see a dragon such as himself again. It has been longer than I think one remembers having dragons lounging in the kingdom."

"I'm going to be here more often, Donka, so

don't let the others wear themselves out while I'm about. There is no reason for them to fuss about me when I'm staying in this realm. I will be a man as much as I can, but it is wonderful to be able to be a dragon when I please, too. And my pretty mate enjoys him too." He looked at Amy when she snorted. "You don't like my dragon?"

"You're nothing like…I don't mean to say that you're not pretty, you are as a dragon, but you're nothing like I've seen in books. That didn't come out right." She looked around before looking back at him. "You're very monstrous looking. No, no, that's not right either. What I mean is that you're not something that would be called warm and fuzzy. All the horns you have over your face and body are quite frightening. And I might well be afraid of you if I didn't know you'd not harm me. You won't, will you?"

"Never. I'd die before I'd ever wish to harm you. And the reason that I'm frightening-looking is because I'm supposed to be. Before I was born, we were the keepers of the timeline. Still are to some extent. Long before my parents were born, we, my family, were there to make sure that the timeline was good for humans. You've no idea how many times we've had to go in and change things to ensure that humans would continue to be. Without them, like magic, we'd not be here either." She asked him if he'd taken it out that humans had seen his kind. "We have. Many times. When there is a great catastrophic event in their world, we will go there to fix things. Stop earthquakes from happening. Put out fires, even at times, start them so that their world is there for them. Also, there have been times when we've had to erase entire generations of humans so that the world as they know it would be a much better place."

"You mean Grail." He nodded and told her that there had been others like him, too. "I guess I can see that. I don't know why you'd bother at times. Humans, even myself included, have fucked up the world enough with our damage to the world."

"It would have been much worse without us." She turned to look out over the field and didn't say anything. "Grandmother invited us over for dinner tonight. I hope you're all right with us going. She had one of the faeries get her a grill, and she's going to try to cook on it. I told her that I'd do it if she didn't mind, and she looked so relieved that I think that might have been her plan all along."

"She loves having you here." He told her that

she loved having her there as well. "She's brilliant, did you know that? I mean, there is nothing that she doesn't know about. Even when we were going over some of the changes to the book, she was able to explain things to me that I didn't understand. She didn't get frustrated with me either about it."

Amy thought about what he'd talked to his grandmother about when he'd been visiting her just yesterday. She'd been telling him that if they wanted, the two of them could go on home. However, he found that he didn't want to leave. Not ever now that he had such a good relationship with not just her but Amy as well. And they were having fun figuring out how much they had in common with not just Amy but his grandmother as well.

"She wants us to go home." She didn't want to go back, he could tell, so when he asked her what she wanted to do, she turned and looked at him. The tears in her eyes made his heart hurt. "I don't want to leave here. Not ever and not be able to return. It's been like an awakening for me. To be loved and to love someone. I have fallen in love with you. And your family, but I have such memories created here that I can't bring myself to leave and not be able to create more of them. Does that make sense?"

"It does. And I agree with you. I don't want to go home, either. There is nothing keeping us from staying here. I honestly think that she only wants us to leave because she thinks that is what we want to do. And doesn't want to tell us for some reason." Amy asked him if he really thought that. "Yes. She's enjoying having us here as much as we love being here. I don't think she wants us to leave either but is giving us an out."

"You think so?" He nodded. "Then we'll tell her what we want when we see her tonight."

They walked over to the castle when it was time to go. Fowler so loved having Amy's hand in his own and took every opportunity that he could get to touch her. They'd been making love every night since the first night, and he found that even the simplicity of holding her was satisfying enough for him. He, at times, thought of how much time he had wasted in being such a fucking dick to her that he at times wished that he could start over. But then, he'd not have what he had now. Which was more than he could have ever hoped for in a mate. He would wish this feeling for everyone in the world.

Grandmother was happy to see them, he could tell. It wasn't as if he'd not seen her several times today, but she was forever happy to see them. As he finished putting the things that she'd prepared on the grill, they sat outside on her lawn and enjoyed the evening. There was so much going on around the land that it wasn't possible to be bored. He loved it here.

"Fowler and I have come to a decision. I hope you are on board with it." He nodded at Amy when she glanced at him. "We don't want to leave. I know that you think that you're holding us here for some reason, but I've never been happier than I am when I wake up in the morning knowing that you're just down the way from me, and I can, whenever I want, go and see you."

"You'll want to leave soon enough. When the children come. Your mother, Fowler, will want to be there for them too." Fowler told his grandmother that Mom could and would come here as much as she wanted and not leave if she didn't want to go. "True. I don't know where she got all her stubbornness from. Certainly not me."

"Right. You're not the least bit stubborn." They all three laughed, and when they were filling their plates with food, Grandmother had a table brought to them so that they could enjoy the outdoors for a bit more. "This is something that I've been thinking about too, Morning. I don't know shit about having a dragon as a baby, so I'm going to depend on you to help me. I know that Storm will as well, but living here with you, we'll be able to raise our children to be free. We won't be able to do that in the other world."

"You want to have children?" Amy nodded, and then Grandmother looked at him. "They'll be dragons, you know that, don't you? Wait. Scratch that. Who knows what your children will be when they're born. I think that Amy has broken more rules on what will happen than anyone that I've ever known. I love that, too."

"We want to live here. Both of us want to be here. Not just for you, though, that is a big factor in this, but because we can be what we want. Do whatever we wish with our magic. Amy is still learning what she can do with what she got from me, and that is something that we'd never be able to figure out if we were living in the other world. Besides that, I think that you and I have spent enough time apart, and I wish, with all my heart, that I could do it all over and come here forever. I love you, Grandmother. With all my heart. Amy has, in the short time that she's been a part of our lives has made me realize that I'm as happy as I will ever be with you and her in my life."

It wasn't quite dark when they headed back to their home. Fowler thought about the fact that they didn't have much room in their home, but for now, he was all right with that. They spent so very little time in their own home and most of it in the yard that he was all right with that. But he knew they'd have to make changes when the children, hopefully soon, came along for them. He thought about Amy being with child and felt an excitement that he'd not ever felt before.

"I don't think she believes that we really want to stay here." Fowler agreed with Amy when she spoke to him in the darkness of their room. "We'll just have to convince her by staying, I guess."

When Amy was asleep, he got up out of bed and made his way to the yard. He wasn't going to shift tonight but work on some of the magic that he'd gotten from Amy when they'd bonded. Just as he was thinking about what to do first, his brother joined him in the yard. He asked Madison if everything was all right.

"I don't know how to answer that." That surprised Fowler, and he told him that. "Good. You might be able to help me if what I'm thinking is true.

You're staying here, aren't you?"

"Yes. We have to convince Grandmother of it, but yes, we want to stay here." He asked about his house. "You want it? Then you can have it. When we go there to visit, we can stay with Mom and Dad. But I don't see us staying much longer than a few days. Amy wants to have my children. I'm in love with her, and she loves me."

"Well, dumb ass, everyone can see that. Yes, I'll take your house. I have some ideas about it that I want to incorporate into it." Fowler waited for his brother to say something more. When he didn't, Fowler told him about the things that he and Amy had talked about with their grandmother. "I've been thinking about finding a mate. I don't want to be like you when you found Amy, but I'm not sure how happy I'm going to be with finding her. Amy can kick your ass and has, I think, on occasion, and I'm not sure how that's going to be with me. I like being in charge of my life."

"What makes you think that you won't be if you find your mate? I mean, things change, of course, but I don't understand why you think you won't be in charge of yourself." Madison told him that she'd want to change him. "And? I don't know if you realize this or not, but you're not perfect. It took me a while to figure out that I wasn't either. She didn't so much as change me, but made me want to change for her. Understand?"

"No. But I want you to think about what you said. You changed. I like me the way that I am. I'm not going to change just because some woman comes along, and I'm going to do anything in my power to make her like me." Fowler couldn't help it. He laughed. "I don't find this to be funny, Fowler. I like me just the way that I am."

"And, just a question here: what makes you think that she's going to want anything different than what you are right now? Also, if she doesn't like the way you are, Amy didn't try and change me. I did that all on my own." Madison said that it was because she had wanted him to be different, or they'd not be together. "I don't understand your logic in that. Not one bit. However, you can't tell what you'll want to do until she comes along. You've not met her yet, have you? And you're trying to get away from her by being here?"

"No. I haven't met her. I don't want to either. I thought about staying here. Forever. Sure, it's to hide out. But I don't care. I don't want to have to change my way of doing anything just because of a woman. And you know what? If she's a human, then I'm all for living out the rest of my life alone. You guys are all I need in the way of family." Fowler couldn't help it. He laughed. And every time he looked at Madison and his sour face, he laughed all the harder. "I don't have any idea why you think this is so funny, but I came here to get advice from you."

"No, you didn't. You came here thinking that I was going to agree with you about having a mate. I have news for you, little brother. You'll want to change when you meet her. I promise." Madison told him he was full of shit. "Perhaps. But not on this. Figuring out what I could have with Amy was the best thing that I've ever had. On top of having someone to love me and be there for me, I have someone that I can talk to about anything."

"And then there is being laid regularly, too, I guess." Fowler just smiled. "Look, don't be all sappy with me and tell me that you'll help me hide out here. I'll go home on occasion. That's why I want your home so that I can hide there if I need to. But I'm not going to go to any functions that might have my mate there. I'm done dating. Period. And I'm never going to go sniffing around for a woman either." Fowler laughed again.

"Madison, I cannot wait for you to meet your mate. I am going to enjoy every minute of you being tamed and made to look foolish when she doesn't want to have a thing to do with you after you've fallen in love. You will, too. I don't know when I wanted Amy to love me back, but I know that I can consider myself to be one of the luckiest men in the world to have her by me." Madison rolled his eyes. "Scoff all you want. But mark my words, you're going to fall and fall hard when she comes around."

"We'll see." The two of them decided to fly the skies together. Madison would bring up how much he wasn't going to change once in a while, and Fowler would laugh at him. But by the time his brother left to go back to the other realm, Fowler's ribs hurt so much he was sure that he was going to be twice as sore tomorrow. But it had been a blast teasing his little brother about his pending mate. He also hoped that she'd come along soon. Everyone could use a good laugh about it, he thought.

Chapter 6

Amy made her way up the mountain carefully. In the morning dew, the grass was slippery, and she didn't want to fall and hurt herself. With having the entire day planned out, getting someone to come and rescue her wasn't on the list.

There were things that she could have picked up on the way up—herbs, flowers to dry, and stones that she thought were very pretty, but she was on a mission, and that mission would keep her from her destination if she picked up too much on the way there. The plot of land that she was heading toward had been one that she'd been dying to get to since she'd heard about it.

"The Valley of Gems isn't too far from here, my lady." She had asked Donka several times over the last few weeks to just call her Amy. To no avail. "Once you have arrived, do you wish my help in getting things set up for you?"

"No, but I do thank you. Fowler is going to join me later this evening, and we're going to set us up a tent and have fun." She didn't understand why the faeries thought that she couldn't set up a tent, but they'd been asking her about it since she and Fowler had planned out this getaway three days ago. "I have the food with me that we're going to have, and all I need to do is warm it up with my magic."

Amy had practiced all day yesterday on 'baking' a potato. She only had to hold one in her hand for seven minutes, and it was done to perfection. However, she did pack them extras in the event that she got nervous and heated them up too much. They were going to be picking up chunks of potato out of the kitchen forever, she thought.

"Who knew that a potato would explode when it got too hot?" Amy looked at Donka, thinking that he was making fun of her, but he looked sincere in his astonishment. The little man had been right there beside her when she had the accident, and he'd been covered in the hot, mushy stuff. Still, she thought it was funny when she thought about Fowler's face when the skin of the tuber had hung from his ears like it had. She was going to remember that for the rest of her life.

"Did I tell you that the Valley has been there for millions of years? It's only been in the last thousand that someone has gone there to look at them." She told Donka that she was excited to see if she could find the gems on her list to bring back for Morning. "Yes, she gave me a list of the herbs we're to look for, too. She has the drying room for them all cleaned. Do you know what she plans with the gems? I have been given permission to take one for my home, my lady. I am so excited to be able to use a beautiful gem from there as my window."

Amy had noticed that a lot of the little people used gems for windows in their homes. It was so beautiful when the sun was shining at just the right angle to make the colors stretch out across the trees and lawns. She was going to see if she could find a cut glass front door for their home to put in just to compete with the faeries.

Once she was at the valley, Amy began setting up things for her and Fowler. The first thing that she did was to start a little fire. A few twigs and she had a hot enough flame to have a nice cup of tea while she got her tent put up. Once she had it right, not taking her nearly as long as she thought it might,

Amy began unpacking the baskets and containers that she'd brought to gather what she'd come for.

The basket that she'd gotten from Morning was just the thing to gather in. Being that it was magical, she could put as much in as she needed to, and it would never be too heavy for her to carry. Storm told her that she could put a car in the basket, and it wouldn't weigh any more than it did while empty. Why she would want to carry a car around wasn't anything that she understood, but it was nice to know just how much she could load in the thing.

Sitting next to the little stream that babbled over the gems that were at the bottom, Amy curled her toes in the water and splashed it over the grass. This was something that she'd never done as a child. Play in a stream barefooted. The closest she'd gotten to doing something so childlike was when she was getting on the bus to school, and it was raining. Stomping her way to the bus and back to the house she'd been living in wasn't even close to the fun and excitement that she was having right now.

Donka showed her how to find the wild herbs that she was to hunt for. It took her several tries to find wild onions. Pulling up grass was funny but not what she needed. When she found heather along the rocks, Amy did a little dance, feeling like a great explorer in the wild. The sun was high overhead when she headed back to the campsite with her findings.

"You did well, my lady. The sage that you found is fragrant, just as it is needed for wraps around wounds." She was learning to use the herbs as much as she was how to find them. It amazed her that the things that she could dig right out of the earth were things that could heal and make a person feel better. Especially when used on a magical creature. "When I was just a baby, my grandmother took lemon verbena and made me tea when I had a cold. The lemon taste became my favorite, and I even use it on my own children."

"I didn't know you had a family, Donka. I'm not keeping you from them too much, am I?" He pointed to the tree line just a few yards away, telling her that his wife and children were there gathering herbs, too. "You must not need much, I would think. If your wife would like some of what I've gathered, please tell her to take them."

"My wife is the one that mixes the herbs for our pip." Amy found out yesterday that a pip, what they call a group of faeries, can be as many as two or thousands. The one that was nearest to her and Fowler's home was quite large as several hundred of them. "Her grandmother and mother before her were the ones that kept the pip well for many years. Her father, he's the leader of ours. He's a good and strong faerie that keeps us working and safe."

Fowler had been telling her all kinds of things about living in a magical world. Not only did they have a constant temperature, but they had foodstuffs, too. There were trees, too, that produced fruit year-round so that the faeries and the dragons could eat them as much as they wanted. The fruit, too, was used as a sweetener in their drinks and desserts.

"Also, you might not be aware of this, but when one of my scales falls off, which is more often than one realizes, they're used for all kinds of things. Weaponry for sure, but they are also used for doors to homes as well as roofs." She asked him how they were cut. "While on the body of our dragons, it's nearly impossible to cut through our scales. However, when one of them falls from our bodies, there is a time, about three days, when they are flexible and soft enough to be cut into shapes. After that, they're so hard that nothing can penetrate them. That's why they make good roofs. A blowing storm cannot knock them off their homes."

He told her how they would find the scale and cut it down. While it's still soft enough, holes were drilled into them for the nails that will hold them secure. Also, cuts would be made for windows and flattened by heavy stones to make them straight. He told her how he'd seen where some of the masters to the scale craft would cut them down into swords and arrowheads for the warriors, too.

"You've seen how they are used first hand." She told him that she'd spoken to those faeries that had drawn their swords on her, and everything was fine. "Yes. They came to me shortly after you spoke to them to tell me what a great and gentle queen you'd be. I wonder if they realize that you wouldn't have hesitated to order their deaths if things had gone the other way."

"I guess we'll never know then." She had smiled at Fowler then. He laughed hard when she winked at him. As they were getting ready for other meetings that day, she reminded him several times that she wasn't a pushover. Amy wasn't sure what he'd do if she were ever under attack. Sometimes, it frightened her when she thought of the damage that might have come to all of them that day.

When the sun was going down, she'd gathered everything on her list of herbs. She'd been shown how to string them up on long sticks so they could be taken into the drying rooms right away and get started on them being readied for use. The gems that Donka and his family gathered, quite a few of them were diamonds that would make windows in their home were being polished by the children.

"We'll set them out so that our children can slide down them as a child would a slide. It's a fun game for them and a way for our gems to be polished enough to be used. Just last week, they were playing on a blue gem. We're sending it to the queen when it's ready. She has expressed a desire for a blue pendant to wear in the summer months."

Donka and Queen Morning were very close. Amy loved to hear stories that the two of them would tell her. Donka would usually make the queen out to be something more than she wanted, and Morning would talk about Donka like he was the best thing that had ever happened to the faerie world. Amy loved them both so much.

Amy had gathered enough gems to fill the new window in their home. Lying them out on the grass, making sure that she had enough for the size, Fowler, as his dragon landed on the grasses beside it. As he stared at the stones the way that she had them laid out, he asked her to move a couple of them and then lifted her up with his clawed hand so that she could see what he'd done.

"It's the forest. And look. You've put the stream in it." She could see that the blue sapphires blended well with the green of the emeralds. The trees seemed to come alive when the sun hit them just right. He had also had her move around the sapphires in the stream to blend well with the purple amethyst and red rubies to have the reflection of the gems sparkle in the stream-like area. "This will be the perfect memory of our day here when this is set up. I love it. I love you, Fowler."

It didn't take them long to have their meal. She'd managed to catch a couple of fish in the deeper part of the stream that she cooked with her magic. Some of the herbs she'd picked up had given the salmon a wonderful flavor, and she couldn't wait to be able to use fresh herbs in all her cooking.

"I thought you didn't like to cook." Amy glared at Fowler when he reminded her what she'd said before coming to this land. "I'm not complaining. You've made some fantastic meals for us. I love the fact too that you can cook us up some popcorn without having to leave the couch."

The two of them were having so much fun being a couple that she sometimes forgot that they hadn't liked each other at the first start. Now, as it was for most couples that she knew, she couldn't imagine a life without him. And didn't want to go on if something were to happen to him where he would leave her. Amy loved him that much.

As they were getting ready for bed, she heated up several large stones with her hands to keep them warm through the night. It wasn't cold, not really, but the chill in the air was enough to keep her awake. Heating the stones was no problem, and the faeries benefited from their warmth as well. Amy fell asleep lying on Fowler's chest and thought that she could stay this way forever.

~*~

"I'm sorry. I don't understand what it is you're saying. I understand the words but not what it is you're talking about. I don't have a sister. Nor do I have any idea where you might have gotten your information about me having one." Layla looked around at the men seated at her kitchen table. "Well? Are you just going to sit there and act like I didn't just tell you that I have no one left that I'm related to?"

"Ms. Jacobson, several months ago, you filled out a DNA test for one of the ancestry places." She told him, again, that she hadn't done that. "Well, we have it on good authority that you did. It turned out that you have not just a sister, but you have a grandmother as well."

They'd been saying the same thing to her for the last two hours. Layla had only just gotten to bed after working a twelve-hour shift at the hospital when they pounded on her door. When she opened her door to figure out why the fuck someone would be wanting to talk to her at nine in the morning, they entered her home without her permission and began pulling out paperwork that was still lying all over her table.

"Look. I'm exhausted and need to get some sleep. Either agree with me that I didn't do this DNA thing and get out, or simply get out. I don't know where you get off telling me this shit anyway. I've been around for the last twenty-five years alone, and I don't need a family at this point in my life." The man who seemed to have the most to say said that they had to clear things up. "I have cleared it up. If you have a problem with it, then I don't give a shit. Get out now, or I'm going to call the police and have you removed."

"Don't you want to know what they left you?" She asked him if they'd died. "Yes. The two of them were in a car accident, and both were killed instantly. "It's quite a large sum of money. As well as other things that are now yours." Something occurred to her, and she glared at the man in front of her.

"So these people knew about me enough to put me in their will, and yet this is the first time that I'm hearing about them. Is that correct?" The man, she didn't know his name and wasn't at all concerned with learning it said that they had all her life. "And they never thought to contact me in any way? Never once reached out and said, hey, we're related? That is a pretty shitty thing to do if you ask me. I could have used a couple of relatives when I was growing up. What is their excuse for not, I don't know, reaching out to say 'hi' or something like that?"

"They didn't want to disrupt your life." Layla nodded, then stood up. "It's all right here if you would allow us to tell you about it. As I said, there is quite a substantial amount of money for you. Wealth beyond your wildest dreams, young lady."

He seemed pissy to her, and she found that her own temper was getting the best of her.

"Get out." The man started to protest, she was sure, and she went to her door and opened it. "I said to get out. If you don't leave by your own power, then I'm going to be forced to help you out of here."

They didn't bother gathering up the paperwork that was still strewn all over her table. The man in charge tried to hand her his card, telling her to contact him when she was in a better frame of mind, but she didn't take it. He ended up laying it on the table and telling her that she was missing out on a great deal of money.

When they were all gone, she sat in her living room, too pissed off now to go back to bed and steamed. Her head was hurting so badly that she was sure it was going to take her days to get it under control again.

Pulling her phone out of her pocket, she did a search on the names that she'd been given as her relatives. She was surprised to find out that they had both been killed only a week ago and had been buried just four days ago. Reading about the accident, she was nearly to the end of the article when someone knocked on her door again. Getting up, pissed about as much as she'd been in some time, she jerked the door open and stared at the man standing there.

He was candy on a stick. Layla had no idea where that thought had come from, but she thought that her imagination had it right. He was tall, about three inches taller than her own six foot, and well built. She knew this because the shirt he had on formed to every curve and muscle that it was holding. His hair, dark brown, looked to have been styled by his fingers and not in an 'I wanna look wind tossed' sort of way but more like he'd run his fingers through it so many times — in what she assumed was frustration — and it still looked good. Licking her lips, her mouth suddenly dry, she got ahold of herself and glared at him.

"What do you want?" He asked her if she had a phone he could use. "And you don't? You do know that every person in the world, even babies still in diapers, has a cell phone attached to their face. Why pray tell don't you have one?"

"I have one, but I tossed it across the road when I had an accident. The fucking tow company said it would be several hours before they could get to me." She asked him why he didn't just pick it up and use it. "Because not that it's any of your business, someone drove over it before I could get to it. Can I use your phone or not?"

"Not." She slammed the door and went back to the couch. "I've had enough of men treating me like I'm dirt on their shoes today. Mother fuckers."

The pounding at her door had her screaming. She didn't normally do that, scream out her frustrations like that, but she figured that today was a good day to start. Going to the door when the prick kept pounding on it. She opened it and was knocked back on her ass when something or someone hit her full in the chest.

Flying backward gave her no time to react. When she hit her head on the table that was behind her, she felt it like it had hit her in the forehead, too. Before she could react, not that she knew what she'd do, the big man was lying across her with his arms wrapped around her. But they weren't arms. Were they wings?

She didn't move when she heard gunfire. The man moaned but didn't let her go. Layla was sure that he'd been killed when he lifted his head and looked down at her. There was so much anger in his eyes that she found herself slightly afraid of him.

"Don't move." She nodded. "You've pissed

someone else off today, I'm guessing. That's why you're a target for whoever fired at you."

"I didn't piss…well, I did, but surely attorneys wouldn't shoot at me if I didn't take their telling me that I have long-lost relatives? Would they?" She was suddenly set free. While she stared at the man from the floor, he looked like a regular person. "You had wings. I saw them. You wrapped me up in them to… you kept me from being killed."

"I don't know what you're talking about. People don't have wings. You must have hit your head." She sat up and watched him as he wandered around her living room. "Where the hell is your phone? The sooner that I'm out of here, the better things will be."

"It's in the kitchen. I don't have a cell phone." She pointed to the kitchen when he asked her again where it was. "You're welcome. Shall I help you off the floor, miss?"

Layla wasn't thrilled that she was talking to herself. She'd done it a long time ago, talking to herself when she was stressed. It had taken her a long time to get out of the habit. Now, here she was doing it again and didn't care that people were making her have bad habits again. Getting up off the floor, she looked at the pillow that had the stuffing hanging out of it. Looking around, she found six, what she assumed were bullet holes around her living room and in her furniture. When the man came out of her kitchen, he sat down on the only chair that wasn't shot up.

"They'll be here in twenty minutes." She asked him to go out and wait in his car. "It's wrecked. Don't you pay attention when someone speaks to you? By the way, you're supposed to go to court tomorrow, or the attorney you pissed off is going to get all that money. It's a great deal of it."

"You snooped in my things? Christ, don't you have any manners?" He didn't answer her but did lay his head back and close his eyes. Kicking him in the foot, he glared at her and asked her what she wanted. "How much?"

"Forty million. That's just in money. I didn't get to read all of it, but there are some properties along with some investments. I'd have to get online to check the prices for today to give you a good accounting. Don't let them take the money. While I don't have any idea what sort of person would leave you money, but the attorneys will get it all, and you'll get nothing." She sat down. Layla was sure that he was still talking, but all she could hear was forty million. Looking at him, she asked him if it was forty million in dollars. "What else would it be? Pennies? Christ, you really did hit your head. Yes, it's dollars. You need to find someone to keep an eye on you. You're not very smart, are you?"

"As a matter of fact, I'm supposed to be brilliant. I have a doctorate in two medical fields. I know eight languages, and I'm fluent in smart ass. Or so I've been told. What's your excuse for being a fucking bastard? Someone shit in your oatmeal this morning. No, that can't be right. You're much too good at being a bastard for it to have just happened." He said she was a smart ass. "I freely admit that. However, I'm not in the best of humor today, so it comes out more."

"You're just stubborn enough to let that money go to waste, aren't you? Christ, you could just take it and spread it around to families that need some helping hand." She told him she'd not decided what she was going to do. "I might just show up to see how you handle yourself. It might be the most entertaining thing that has happened to me of late."

Going to her door, for the second time today, she was tossing someone out of her home. Her head was pounding so hard that she was getting tunnel vision. And this arrogant ass wasn't making it any better. When she felt something trickle down the back of her neck, she reached up to see if her hair had come loose. As soon as she looked at her hand, she knew that she was in big trouble.

"You're bleeding." She stared at the man. His face was becoming fuzzy as she watched him. "Did you hear me? You're bleeding. What the hell is wrong with you that you don't even know —"

"I want you to get out of my house. I'm fucking sick to death of you calling me names." He said again that she was bleeding. "Really? Is that what all this red stuff is that I have on my head. Well, aren't you just about the most helpful shithead that I've ever known?" She pointed to the door, or at least she hoped that she was. "I want you out of here right now."

Layla was getting sicker by the moment. If she passed out in front of this person, she knew that he'd just leave her on the floor to die. Telling him again to get out, she held onto the back of her couch to keep herself upright. But it wasn't working. She was falling forward even as the fucker was grabbing her.

"I'm not going to save you. You're not going to

be anything to me, do you hear me?" If she answered him, she didn't remember. Everything was hurting now, and she didn't know if she was going to be able to close her door when he left her alone. If he left her. Things were moving too quickly for her to make sense of anything at the moment.

"Madison, she's lost a lot of blood." She didn't know the other voice, but it was just pissy enough that she knew that it had to be a person that was related to shithead. "Are you going to do anything?"

"No. He's going to leave me alone." She knew she'd said that out loud as both men turned to look at her. While she didn't know where she was, Layla knew that she wasn't at her home anymore. "I want you both to get out of my house and leave me alone. I want to die in peace."

"You're not at your home. Now shut up and let the doctor see to your head. You should have said something about being hurt." She thought about his wings and how they'd kept her from being shot. "I don't have wings. You're just off your rocker enough to tell someone that you saw them. I don't have them. Now, close your mouth and let the doctor fix you up."

Layla knew the voice that was yelling at the

man. It was her boss, Doctor Sheppard. When she felt the pinch at her arm, the feeling of floating slid over her, and she let the drugs take her under. Reaching for her friend, Sheppard told her that she was going to be just fine. Just fine, indeed.

"I heard you telling patients that when they were dying. That's not too terribly encouraging right now." Laughter. She didn't know from whom, but it made her smile. "I never knew you had such a sexy laugh before. Hey, don't let that man come in here. He's mean, and I don't like him."

"I don't like you either, but that's not going to matter much in the long run, now is it?" That was as confusing as she had ever heard, and she thought about telling the man that. "Listen, you have to lie still. He can't stitch you up when you're moving around like a rabbit trying to find his hole."

"Don't be a doctor. You have no bedside manner at all. I thought I told you to go away." He said that she was holding his hand. "Well, I don't want to do that either. Go away."

However, she couldn't let go of his hand. For some unknown reason, she was getting some comfort from it. Security came to mind as well. When Sheppard told her that he was going to give her a bit more juice this time, there was no way she was going to be able to speak. Every part of her body was relaxed enough that she was sure someone had taken out all her bones.

Tomorrow, she was going to have to go to court and figure out how she had a family. Her last thought was that the man was somehow going to be related to her too, and wouldn't that have been like the monkey calling her mom.

"Go to sleep. What the hell is a monkey calling your mom about?" Layla felt her mind simply shut down. If she answered shithead, she didn't care. The fucker could go to hell for all she cared.

Before You Go...

HELP AN AUTHOR

write a review

THANK YOU!

Share your voice and help guide other readers to these wonderful books. Even if it's only a line or two, your reviews help readers discover the author's books so they can continue creating stories that you'll love. Log in to your favorite retailer and leave a review. Thank you.

Kathi Barton, a winner of the Pinnacle Book Achievement Award and a best-selling author on Amazon and All Romance books, lives in Nashport, Ohio, with her husband, Paul. When not creating new worlds and romance, Kathi and her husband enjoy camping and going to auctions. She can also be seen at county fairs with her husband, an artist and potter.

Her muse, a cross between Jimmy Stewart and Hugh Jackman, brings her stories to life for her readers in a way that has them coming back time and again for more. Her favorite genre is paranormal romance, with a great deal of spice. You can visit Kathi online and drop her an email if you'd like. She loves hearing from her fans. aaronskiss@gmail.com.

Follow Kathi on her blog: http://kathisbartonauthor. blogspot.com/